The House on the Rocks

ALEXA DONLEY

First paperback edition October 2023

Book design by Danna Mathias Steele

ISBN 979-8-9874803-0-4 (paperback)

ISBN 979-8-9874803-1-1 (ebook)

www.alexadonley.com

She stands at the top of the cliff.

Closes her eyes to the ancient house behind her, tall and regal and full of memories she will never know or understand; the beach far below her, the dirt and pebbles her feet dislodge from the unstable cliffside hitting the boulders at its base; the waves rolling far below, spray reaching up toward her like grasping hands, the brine sharp enough she'll smell it for days; the gray ocean stretching far in the distance until the horizon curves and meets the sunlight so that she feels like she's looking down a long tunnel; the beat of the waves and the salt of the air and the wind in her dress fading away until she's just breathing. Just being.

And then she feels the hand on her shoulder.

Chapter One

The garage sale was mostly garbage, but Meg was certain there was treasure too.

It was the end of the summer, but that didn't mean that it had gotten any cooler; she could feel the sun frying the back of her neck as she leaned over the cardboard box at her feet. A drop of sweat trickled down the side of her face, and she brushed it away, wiped it on her pants, and focused. This box was just sweaters; there was nothing handmade, nothing too well-loved, no tags or notes... She moved onto the next box, realizing at the last minute that someone else had been looking, too. She glanced up to apologize but they were already leaving—giving up.

Meg wasn't giving up. There were *stories*, here. Clamoring, vibrant, living stories, demanding to be unearthed. If she only dug deep enough, pulled on the right leads, she could find them; the quest of it filled her. A responsibility, almost.

They were waiting for her.

She batted a stray fly off the edge of the box, tuned out the familiar soundtrack of cars idling and the heavy air pressing on her bent shoulders, and dug to the bottom. Elbow-deep in someone's pile of old shirts, the sweat beading on the back of her neck this time, her hair clinging to her forehead so that the curls flattened out, she tuned in only to what her fingers touched, what she smelled, the odd colors that mixed together like a washing machine turning.

What was interesting? What was different? What was someone's, once, that they had cherished and loved, and now it was here for her to love just as much?

Meg tilted the box sideways to move the shirts she had already looked at out of the way, turned them over like a baker kneading bread. The scratch of faded t-shirt graphics and wool against her arms, the smell of dust and sweat and old perfume and the salt of the sea nearby that got into everything, the unraveled threads that snagged in her nails when she pulled them free... A sequin caught on the edge of her finger, and she focused there, taking a handful of shirts out so she could see better.

But it was only a girl's tank top, one she was pretty sure she had seen at the mall when they drove into Port Angeles last week. Not as interesting as she had hoped for when she started to excavate for it. All it told her was that the elderly man leaning against the garage definitely didn't own this box. She hadn't seen anything that could be his yet; it seemed he was just the unlucky person who got to host the sale. He caught her looking and narrowed his eyes at her through the cloud of white smoke around his head, raising the cigarette to his lips again.

Next to him, her friend Beth stepped out of the shade of the garage and speed-walked toward her. "I'm dying," she rasped, pulling her braids back out of her face and into a loose ponytail. Meg had told her she should just cut her hair when it had finally slid from spring into the late Washington summer and the temperature climbed, but she was persistent. The only person Beth was guaranteed to listen to was herself—and sometimes even that was questionable.

"Why don't you at least put it up?" she suggested.

Beth blinked at her a second, then shook her head. "No, not that. The smoke. How the hell do you smoke when it's *this hot?*"

"I asked you that when you put on jeans instead of shorts. Remember?" Meg put the shirt back and moved on to the stacks of books and movies next to it. She picked up a trilogy, the pages dog-eared and spines pulling apart, and flipped through the first few pages of each book. Nothing in the first one, nothing in the second one, *to Pam love Mom* in the third... She looked in the back, but there was nothing more so she set it down and moved on. Sometimes there was a pattern to the books or movies themselves, but those were secondhand treasures; she couldn't take them with her, just as a photo on her phone. One of her favorites: every edition of Sherlock Holmes, book and movie and spinoff, in one box labeled *free to anyone who can tell me Sherlock's mother's name*. There was a whimsical fancy to it that Meg had loved, and she was tempted to look it up but that felt like cheating. It was enough. Just the picture made her smile.

"I asked *you* that when we left the house." She paused, glancing at the sequin top. "Are we going clubbing?"

"Har har. Help me look."

Beth didn't question her. Just started fishing through tapes opposite where Meg was working, so they could work twice as fast without overlapping, and Meg felt her chest expanding with a fierce warmth. They had a *system*. For all her complaining, she could count on Beth.

She bit down her smile—a little too wide for rummaging through garage sale leftovers, too private—and flipped through the tapes in the next box. Tapes, not DVDs, which was why she was bothering at all. Tapes were older, and couldn't be bought at the mall and dumped on a whim, and that had potential.

Beth glanced up, over her shoulder, and then back down. "There's a boy behind us who hasn't taken his eyes off you the whole time we've been here."

Meg restrained the urge to look up and behind her. "In a good way?" Stupid question. "What does he look like?"

"Hmm... like a good one-night stand?" When Meg made a face, she grinned brightly to show she was kidding, cast a casual look over her shoulder, and then ducked back down. "Brown hair. Green eyes. Looks like he does track and plays video games in his free time."

"Ugh," Meg said, then prayed he hadn't heard. Since Beth didn't immediately start dying of laughter, she decided she'd take that as a no. "Why don't *you* go after him?"

"Because you need a little adventure in your life!"

"I have adventure a-plenty," Meg said, turning her attention back to the video tapes. Mostly kids' movies. Boring. "Have you found anything interesting?"

"*No.*"

Meg glanced up at her tone of voice; Beth looked mostly amused, but also exasperated. "Meg," she said. "I love you. I really do. But you're like a grandma."

"You think I should jump from garage sales to one-night-stands with strangers?"

"Maybe he likes going through other people's clothes, too. Never know."

Meg grinned and threw the sequined top at her; Beth squeaked and swatted it away. Behind her, the smoking man grunted in disapproval, like he knew he was supposed to stop them but didn't have the energy.

"You ask him out," she told Beth. "If you want adventure so much…" Her fingers paused on one of the tapes just as she almost skipped past it; it looked newer than the others, and Meg pulled it from the box and examined it. It had no design on the cover or spine, plain and unremarkable, but when she pulled out the tape itself to find the label, in marker someone had written *1.*

A video someone had made for themselves. Maybe something generic… but maybe a treasure that could rival a photo album.

"Oh no. I know that look. What'd you find?" Beth had walked to her side of the table while she was preoccupied, and she peered closer at it. "Is that a home video?"

"Maybe," Meg said, trying to keep the smile off her face and failing. "I mean, I don't know why someone would give away their home videos—"

"You've found wedding dresses and baby pictures."

"True. Maybe it's just a video, but…" She shrugged, but couldn't help the excitement that welled up inside of her and spilled out in an exhilarated laugh. Imagine what she could *find* on this. There was nowhere people were more genuine than on video, especially candid, unedited, old video. Maybe it was a vacation with a family, with embarrassing parents and siblings and one unfortunate person manning the camera. Maybe it was a wedding, with well-wishes and toasts and first dances. Maybe it was a video of someone they loved, talking about an anniversary or trip or event, or the camera was set up as the unsuspecting person was led to a special spot so they could get down on one knee...

"I know that look, too." Beth pulled the box toward her so they could share. "Let me guess, you want to know if there's more of them."

Meg laughed again, pleased. "You know me so well," she said. "And for someone who thinks I need more action in my life, you're the best enabler."

"You make it sound like I'm getting you drugs, woman," Beth grumbled, but she stayed and helped her sort through them anyways.

Out of the whole lot, they found four more blank videos, labeled in order of how they were made; Meg could hardly hold them when she took them over in a stack to the man at the garage, who begrudgingly sat up. That was a bonus. She wanted to know more about these finds, and usually older people were willing to indulge her where people her age weren't.

She dug in her jeans pocket and handed him ten dollars. "Keep the change," she told him with a smile. Usually that was enough to get at least a smile in return, maybe loosen their lips, but the man just put it in the book at his side like a bookmark.

Annoying, but only a minor setback. Meg cleared her throat and tried again. "So are these yours?"

The man grunted. "Everyone's."

"Well yes, but—"

"I don't know," he said impatiently, blowing smoke into the heat around them; Meg held in a cough that would definitely make him stop talking until her lungs hurt with the strain. "They dropped stuff off. I'm just sittin' here."

She felt it, like a physical reaction: heat under her skin, her throat starting to itch with the words she was holding back. There was *no reason* for him to be that rude when she was just asking a logical question. "I just want to know—"

"Thank you," Beth said quickly, grabbing Meg's arm and hooking it through her own, steering them both away so abruptly she almost stumbled and dropped the precious tapes. "You've been *so* helpful. Have a good day."

They set off walking quickly; just as quickly as her anger had arisen, it dissipated, left behind only embarrassment. God, she was so glad Beth stopped her—although it was a little surprising, too. "You were unusually helpful, there," she grumbled.

"Too hot to start shit." Beth patted her arm. "As funny as that would have been, you letting him have it, you would've regretted it."

Meg sighed. "You do know me."

"And, you know, we have his address, so if you want we can come back later and do something to get in his head. Maybe bring him a McDonald's he didn't order and say it's from his girlfriend, or drop off a whole stack of newspapers overnight..."

And there she was. Meg laughed, patting her on the arm to let her know it was okay. Usually, she and Beth fit in each other's personalities, but her parents used to tell her stories about when they teamed up when they were younger. *You acted like sisters,* they laughed, even though Beth was more muscular and had darker skin and drew people's eyes so much more that she had never thought that was true. *When the two of you were on the same page, when you* **both** *decided you needed to go on a certain trip or someone was being bullied... Look out!*

She didn't do that, anymore; there weren't as many battles to fight, in adulthood, when you made your own choices. But it was better that way, she thought. She didn't like her temper, so she was glad that Beth was reasonable when she forgot to be. She liked to follow Beth's vibrant light instead of casting her own.

"He wouldn't remember it, anyway." Meg shouldered up her purse, bulging with the tapes. She couldn't wait to watch them and see what they had found, this time. It made the cranky old man and the heat and the time worth it. "I appreciate the thought, though. Warms my heart."

Beth nudged her, hard enough she tripped off the sidewalk, and pretended to be upset when Meg nudged her back. "Come on," she said, casting a glance at the sky above them. "Let's go before the weather changes."

"Mm." Meg tipped her head back and looked up. It didn't look like rain, but it felt sticky hot. As if they could suffocate under the clouds and the sunlight combined, a silent storm that she liked far less. "Yeah. Come on. Air-conditioning will be nice."

She let Beth lead her back to the car, clutching the tapes so she didn't accidentally break them. Whatever was on here, it was important to somebody once—and now it could be important to her.

Chapter Two

Meg liked to brace people to see her apartment by telling them it was 'eclectic' or 'lively,' but the best word now was 'secondhand.' She was losing track of the individual finds, with how many places and years she had found them, but almost everything she had found at a garage sale and had to bring back, and whenever she held the pieces in her hands she got to discover the stories all over again.

Some of her favorites and her new finds she didn't even want to put away yet. Right now, when she opened the door, it made music—the doorknob was the only place she had found for the charming hummingbird wind chime she bought last week. The lady who sold it to her had brightened, on the verge of proud tears, when she brought it up to buy it. Her daughter had made it, and she had made better ones since then but that had been the first step toward her dream of being an artist. It made Meg smile now, hearing its soft tones, knowing why one of the wings was bigger than the other.

"*Air conditioning,*" Beth said dramatically, flopping down on the couch. The motion sent several books crashing to the ground, and she pushed another one off half-heartedly. "You're killing me with your habit, you know."

"You can move out any time, whiner." Meg scooted carefully through her piles to their old video player; Beth made herself comfortable on the couch, because by now she just knew that if there was something good on these Meg wasn't moving for hours. She had back-to-back shifts tomorrow and the next day—being a waitress didn't pay much, especially for a mom-and-pop burger joint, but it made rent—so she would just have to watch as much of these as possible today and resume when she could.

That all hinged on there being something good on here. She just hoped it wasn't porn this time. That had been an awkward dinner.

"I might if you don't let me watch my show," Beth groused, pulling out her yarn and crochet hooks. It was rather brave of her, Meg thought, to call her a grandma when *she* was the one who had taken up crocheting during college and was slowly filling their apartment with socks and hats. "There's a new episode tonight."

"Watch it tomorrow." Meg shushed her, sitting down in front of the TV, setting it up to copy the footage as they watched it. She had lost too many good finds to accidents, and if this was something good, she wanted to make sure she had it to keep. "Are you ready?"

"Ready."

Meg got comfortable in her spot, took a deep breath, and pressed play.

The blank TV switched to footage of the gently rolling sea, stretching out for miles, in a slow pan that reminded her of a cheesy documentary on national parks. Not porn, thank God, but no people like she had been hoping for, even as the seconds stretched on into minutes. Just scenery. It looked like a beach on the Washington coast, but not one she recognized. It had a feel to it. The sea was more temperamental than in other places. Colder.

"Pretty," Beth commented carefully, "But..."

"Hold on," Meg insisted, still watching closely for any sign of action on the silent TV, with stunning vistas of the storm rolling in over a beach made of boulders as big as she was; the camera was shaking now, betraying that it was a camcorder being held. She could see the wind moving over the water, feel the darkness creeping through the picture as the clouds grew thicker and more ominous over the recorder's head, and leaned forward. She had the sound down so low it was silent, but she bet that when she turned it up the wind would buffet the speaker into static with enough force to make her cringe. Maybe she'd look at it later, by herself, and there would be narration. That would give it personality, tell her where it was and whether it was the recorder's first time there.

Beth sighed heavily. "I suppose you think this is worth it."

Of course she did, Meg wanted to answer, *of course she did.* What Beth didn't seem to understand, what nobody seemed to understand no matter how she tried to put it into words, was that people only invested time in things that mattered to them, and it was the things that mattered to them that *made* them. People who painted were careful observers, appreciators of beauty and intrinsic dreamers. People who did sports were competitors in life, brash and unrelenting and unwilling to take no for an answer. People with large families were treasurers of memories, sentimental and devoted, capturing pieces of themselves in people they loved. Their stories were all so different, and so important, and when she found them and saved them in her own memory... they lived forever.

How could that *not* be worth it?

The camera moved faster, now, running along the beach, following the direction of the wind and crashing waves. It was a beautiful beach, empty, with no docks or litter or other people. The tapes were an old medium, but the picture was clear, and when the camera dipped down with a motion sudden enough to turn her stomach the person was in plain white, modern running shoes. So this wasn't as old as she had originally thought, but that only made it more interesting. From the shoes, the person recording looked to be a man. Maybe they would see his face, but not yet.

"Why are they running?" Beth asked. Meg didn't need to turn around to see she was leaning forward, watching with her. It was getting interesting now.

"I guess we'll find out," she answered. She *hoped* they'd find out.

The movement slowed as he neared the edge of the rocks where the waves picked up and washed over them in great white sheets; Meg could feel the power in them. This storm that he was filming was going to be a big one. She hoped he would get out before the sky got any darker, before it became dangerous.

He reached the waves—the camera shuffled to the side for a second, like he had forgotten about it—and then turned forward again. In his hand, the picture focused on a single white sandal, dripping saltwater. It was a flat sandal, with thin straps crisscrossing the sides and the ones that should've gone around the ankle still fastened. There was a flower on top, and he turned it over to the sole that was clean enough it looked like it had just been picked out of a store.

A shiver crawled down Meg's spine, watching him turn it over and study it, and then the camera started to move, looking for the owner. There was no one else on the beach. Maybe it was just trash... but his attention suggested otherwise. Behind her, Beth was silent. Suddenly Meg wished she had the sound on, because even the static of wind hitting the speaker would diminish the sense of foreboding that empty sandal brought crashing over her.

The camera focused back out on the sea (the winds picking up, clouds a blanket over the water) and then the man started down the beach. His progress was slow, but Meg found herself hoping there was a reason for it.

Beth got up, shifting uneasily on her feet, and said faintly, "I'm going to get something to drink."

Liar. She just didn't want to see what they might find.

After a few breathless moments of watching, maybe thirty seconds of the person walking over the boulders as carefully as possible without dropping the camera, they rounded a corner.

There was another person on the beach. A girl with pale skin and long golden hair and a white sundress—like an angel downed by the storm, Meg thought, utterly at odds with the blackening sky and crash of the waves and the first drops of rain beginning to fall. She brushed her hair behind her ear with one hand, laughing in a way that wasn't at the man holding the camera but at herself, and in the other hand she held a matching white sandal so that she was barefoot and braced between two rocks.

The man held out the matching sandal, which she took. *Thank you,* she said, her eyes kind and full of laughter and focused on the camera and the person looking through it.

Meg felt herself smiling again, wider. *This is why I do this.*

She heard Beth come back in. "Ah, a happy ending."

"Yep," Meg said, eyes on the screen. "Good find. You're not getting the TV back for a few days, sorry."

Beth sighed again, but settled in beside her with her yarn to keep watching.

CHAPTER THREE

It was a love story.

She glances up at the camera, over her shoulder, and a smile spreads over her face like it's second nature. She's wearing jeans and a plain sweatshirt, and she hugs her knees to her chest to keep warm. "Well hello there, stranger. Am I being interviewed?"

"Hello to you, too." He sits down heavily next to her, setting the camera on the ground so it faces the sea. It's early- to mid-fall, the sun a distant memory and the clouds whipping into huge towers over the water. "I told myself I'd document things this year, so I'm carrying it around, that's all. I didn't know you were down here this time. I was just going to film the beach."

"Liar," she says lightly, and he laughs, caught. "You never told me where you got that camera, by the way. I didn't know they still made them."

"It was my mom's. I found it while we were cleaning. I figured I might as well use it."

She hums. "So... if you had time to clean, did you have time to read that book I loaned you?"

"Not yet. It's too nice of a day to stay inside. I have to enjoy it before it starts raining."

"Alright, that's a good excuse, I'll give you that one. But you have to read it! I need somebody to talk to about the ending!"

A long pause, where he mulls over his words. Then... "Is it too late to tell you I'm not much of a reader?"

She gasps. He backpedals.

"I mean, I like to read sometimes, I just never really have the time—"

She laughs again, louder, and there's a small crunching sound; rocks fall like she's collapsed from the energy of it. After a split second, he laughs too. "Don't do that to me!"

Their laughter drowns out the ocean.

The camera moves toward her, with her back to it because she's watching the sea. The rain is pelting down, and she's wearing jeans and an enormous jacket that belongs to a man. (Probably his.) Her blonde hair knots in the wind.

He moves slower, and slower, until he's creeping up and the camera is focused on her face as she looks into the distance; she glances over at it, does a double-take and whips backward in surprise. Then she starts laughing.

"Say cheese," he whispers in mock solemnness, and she shoves the camera away.

"Go away!" But she doesn't mean it, and she leans over the camera in a way that can only be to kiss him, and it's a long while before it focuses on something besides their feet again.

It's pouring. The waves are enormous, crashing over the rocks so that they crack against each other like thunder. When the camera pans over the water, the line between the horizon and the edge of the sky is hazy, nearly invisible. There's a

jagged strike of lightning, clear and pronounced and lighting up the sky and edge of a cliff that juts out over darkness—

They count together, barely discernible over the roar of the wind and rain. "One Mississippi, two Mississippi, three..."

Rumbling, starting from in front of them and reverberating on all sides, like a primordial beast waking from sleep. They both whoop and holler, the exhilaration of getting close to something dangerous and forbidden and bigger than them.

The day is finally clear, the sky vast and cloudless and blue, and she stands with her arms thrown out like she's absorbing every single ray of light. "Sun!" she says in a sigh. "Blessed sun! Oh how I've missed you!"

He laughs. "Drama queen."

"Says the man who pulled out his shorts two weeks ago in preparation." She turns and grins at him teasingly, then looks forward again. They're not at the beach, but standing in a beautiful green grass field. In the far distance is a house that looks like it should be in black and white, regal and ancient and on the edge of falling apart. It's three stories tall, with peeling blue paint an octagon turret on one side, windows that look out over the water and an imposing black wrought-iron fence around it, but the camera pans back to her like she's the only interesting thing for miles around.

"Well, I know you missed your sundresses, too. Don't deny it, you did."

"Well, yeah," she says, glancing down at her navy sundress. "And also these."

She lifts up her foot, indicating flat white sandals with a flower on top—the one she lost on the day at the beach with the incoming storm. The one that brought them together when he returned it to her.

"Ah," he says, voice fond. "Yeah. I like those, too."

She grins, brushing her hair behind her ear, and runs forward. "Race you!"

The camera drops sideways in the grass, their laughter in the background.

"So why does the rain keep us from going to the beach?"

"I've broken my ankle on those rocks before. And believe me, once is enough."

She pauses, thinking. "Then where are we going?"

"There's someone I want you to meet."

They're back behind the house—the wrought iron fence is in the distance, the only sign of civilization—and then the camera aims back down at their feet. They're walking through grass, but it's muddy enough that there's suction whenever he takes a step. She's in tennis shoes, too, and walks like the mud doesn't bother her. "Someone lives back here?"

"...No."

And then the grass, still neatly manicured and lush green, turns to a patch of stone. He doesn't pan up to the writing, but there are flowers at its base.

She sucks in a quick breath, nearly lost in the rain. "This is..."

"Yeah." He breathes deep, too. "I wish you could have met her."

The camera turns off. Too private. Too personal.

"Come on, come on, come on!"

She's dragging him down the beach, looking back at him and the camera often enough she nearly falls face-first on the rocks before he catches her.

"What?" he asks, laughing. "What's so important? What's waiting down here?"

She laughs. "Nothing, if we don't hurry." And she does sound a little nervous, urging him faster by tugging on the hand not holding the camera; it skews to the ground, and he doesn't bother to correct it. "I had... a friend bring it down here, and I wanted it to be here since this is where we met and it's been a year and..."

"You're rambling. Whatever it is, you know I'll love it, if it's from you."

"Still—"

"How did your friend even get in here?"

"Just come on!"

They stop moving; there's a moment of breathless silence, nothing but the sea crashing against the rocks.

Then—barking. And he starts laughing in pure joy.

The camera is set down on the rocks, but their feet move away.

"You got me a dog?!"

"Well, you said you wanted one, and I thought, why not? I mean, I just found this ad in the newspaper and this one was the runt of the litter and—"

And then no more talking, for a long moment, and a small golden retriever puppy goes running across the rocks with a red bow around its neck.

She stands at the edge of a cliff, looking out over the calm sea, a white dress and white sandals and her hair down and moving in the slight breeze. The sky isn't gray, like when they first met, but painted with pinks and reds and oranges from the sunset that taint the water beneath it. She stands and admires it, hands hanging at her sides.

The camera moves forward, slowly so as not to disturb her, and the sunlight catches on something on her left hand: a diamond ring. She clasps her hands behind her back and breathes the salty air in deep.

The camera comes up next to her, and she glances at it. There's nothing but peace in her eyes and breathless joy in her smile as she looks at the camera and the person through it, and then she turns back to the water and watches the sun. Everything is still. Silent, asleep, respectful.

The camera retreats a step, looking at her back and the back of her head, and then the hand on her shoulder moves.

Forward.

She gives a little cry of surprise, arms windmilling for half a second, and disappears over the edge of the cliff in a shower of rocks.

There's no yelling. No screaming. Just a dull, wet CRACK.

Meg screamed.

Somewhere else, dimly, she was aware of yelling, over the top of her screaming, and she clasped her hands over her mouth to stop it but she couldn't tear her eyes away from the screen—the edge of the cliff, the beautiful sunset, the still water. It looked beautiful. Perfect. But she knew what was down at the bottom. The rocks that had grown so familiar, jagged and sharp and stained; the white dress red, limbs askew, neck too far to the side, the waves breaking only feet away and taking away blood and the body—

Meg bolted for the bathroom, diving for the closest thing—the sink. Her vision was blurry, and she felt tears running down her face and tasted bile in her throat, and she wanted to scream but everything was stopped up so she just clenched the sink with both hands. When she closed her eyes, she could see it. When she tried to sleep tonight, she would hear the sound of that girl's head breaking against the rocks.

"Meg," Beth asked, sounding a thousand miles away, "Are you okay?"

Murderer, Meg thought, a word she'd seen in stories all her life that had always seemed an abstract term. The cameraman was a murderer. The girl's fiancé was her murderer. That wasn't the way the story was supposed to go. That wasn't the way *her* story was supposed to go.

"It's just a video," Beth murmured. "It's not real."

Only it *was.* She knew it. She'd watched too much for it not to be. She knew the people in the videos as if they were her neighbors, her friends, an extension of herself.

And now one of them was dead.

And the other was a murderer.

Chapter Four

“Tell me again what your name is.”

Meg looked down at her hands on the clean white table and resisted the urge to look at the mirror behind her. She had watched enough TV to know it wasn’t a mirror. Everyone knew. But it still made her fidget, knowing that there were police behind there, watching her every move. They were calling her a witness.

‘Witness’ had much more gravity than ‘unlucky garage-sale shopper.’

“Meg.”

“Full name?”

“Megan Schuller.”

The police officer smiled in an attempt to get her to relax that didn’t work. “I just need you to tell me how you found the tapes.”

“I was at a garage sale.”

“Do you remember where?”

She wasn’t sure she could forget it. “Yes.”

“Do you know who was running it?”

“No. It was a community garage sale. There were at least ten families dropping things off while I was there.”

“And what made you pick up the tapes?”

Back and forth. Back and forth. Meg found herself watching the officer so that she wouldn’t think about the ones she couldn’t see behind her, watching, deciding whether she was reliable. He was perfectly still across the table. They all were, that she had seen so far. They were eager to calm her down, to get her to think logically instead of about the videos. *Distance yourself from it,* he had said, and she wasn't quite sure what that meant. What was the distance you could get from watching someone die? What was the distance between her and the girl who had been so happy and was gone now?

This was real. She felt it. She *knew it.* She had read a lot of stories, watched a lot of movies with love stories and tragedy at the finale, and they hadn't gutted her like this, and that meant it had to be real.

"And you believe the video you saw was real? Not a movie someone made?"

"Do you think I'd bring it here if I wasn't sure?" she demanded, swallowing and blinking rapidly because she still wanted to cry, why did everyone keep *saying that?* "Did you watch it?"

"Yes." His voice was condescendingly gentle. "And I assure you, we are going to investigate it to the fullest extent."

That sounded like goodbye, and sure enough he stood up; Meg didn't, still processing. That couldn't be it. A promise to look into it? "Do you know who she is? Or who he is?" They had called each other by nicknames maybe five times in the footage. 'Liz' and 'Cal.' That was all they were. Two mysteries.

"Not yet. But we'll find out."

"You'll let me know?"

For the first time he stopped, and Meg placed the look on his face easily enough this time: it was confusion. Possibly suspicion. She rubbed her hands together and made herself stop because maybe that was suspicious, too. "I just... want to know."

The man nodded to the door, which opened to let her out. "We'll contact you if we have any more questions, yes."

That wasn't what she meant, but she left anyways.

"Are you going to tell me what your big surprise is?"

"Not yet. Then it wouldn't be a surprise."

She laughs, twines her hands behind her back. She moves over the rocks with deliberate care; they don't even shift under her feet even though they look haphazard and treacherous. She's been down here so many times she knows which ones don't move and steps around the ones that do. "You have a present for me."

He stops short. "How..."

"You don't usually wear a jacket down here. You're 'used to it,' remember? I know you too well!"

"You really do," he says, and it sounds wondrous, almost reverent. "You really do."

"Hello. My name is Meg Schuller. I was in the other day—"

"Yes." The officer at the front desk didn't smile, but the severity of the frown lessened. Only slightly. "I remember. Did you have something else to tell us?"

"No. I was just... wondering whether you know who was responsible yet."

"Not yet." Her voice was curt, enough it was startling. This wasn't like the police officer who had interviewed her in the room, who had told her gently that they were going to look into it with all of their resources—but then, that hadn't been a police officer saying that. That was a first responder's voice, because she had actually been shaking when she went to them with the tapes and told them what she found. In that moment, she was someone who needed their attention.

Now she was someone pushing them for answers they didn't have, and that was a hindrance. An unwelcome distraction.

"I'm sorry. Just... will you let me know if you find anything?"

"We'll contact you if we need another statement."

That wasn't the same thing.

They're sitting on the beach, looking out over the ocean; it's a calm day, and the sun overhead beats down on them. The camera is focused on the horizon, where the breeze stirs up small waves that break up the gray. There are seagulls crying, diving toward the beach and back up, but otherwise it's silent, just the two of them.

"It's like something out of a photograph," she says. "It's so nice."

"We can go if you want—"

"No. If this is important to you, then it's important to me."

And while the scenery is beautiful, the camera turns to her. She's perched on a rock, sitting forward, and she's not looking out over the water—she's staring at him, with fondness, but also with a studying edge. Memorizing what he looks like, here, where he says he's happiest. Figuring out why.

"...It is important to me," he admits.

The smile softens. "Then I want to learn why."

When Beth walked through the door, she nearly dropped the groceries. "What the *hell?*"

Meg didn't really think that reaction was warranted—although she had thought she would be gone for longer, too. Half of her wanted to lunge for the TV, to turn it off, but it was too late. "What?"

"What do you mean, *what?* Why are you watching that? Didn't you give them all the tapes?"

"They didn't ask me if I copied them."

"*Meg.* You... I don't..." She stopped herself, shook her head as if rejecting what she was seeing, and then walked briskly into the kitchen. "It's been a week and a half. *Why?*"

"I don't know, I just..." She turned back to the TV, panning over the lawn. There was a car in the driveway this time, one of the only signs that the tapes were even from the same world. Most of it seemed so removed, so unreal. She couldn't read the license plate. "Wanted to." That wasn't the right word, but she couldn't find the right word. "I don't know."

Beth sighed. "Please at least tell me—"

"I threw that one away."

She's sitting on his bed, cross-legged in jeans and a plain t-shirt. There is a steady drum of rain outside, large fat raindrops that drown out any other sound. The room is mostly bare except for the bed, and the camera angle suggests he's sitting in a chair across the way. It looks less like a bedroom and more like a hotel room—no personalization, no mess, no signs that someone lives there.

She hums and laughs self-consciously, tucking her hair behind her ear. "You know it looks like you're about to interrogate me, with the camera."

"I don't think they use things like this anymore." He laughs once. "Sorry. We haven't seen each other for a week, so..."

"So you wanted to know what you missed?" She leans back on her hands to look at the ceiling, thinking, and then startles and looks to the side. "What was that?"

"What was what?"

"I thought..." She shakes her head, and the smile returns. "Nothing. The wind throws me off sometimes. It feels like it's... alive."

"I told you," he says, and there's a hint of teasing in his voice, "This house has character."

"Meg," the officer at the front desk said, and while her voice was kind enough, her eyes were flint. "I don't have anything new to tell you. We will let you know if we need any more information from you."

Would you? Meg wanted to scream it, but this was a police station and she was in public and there were rules. That classified you as 'hysterical,' screaming in public. No one wanted to deal with hysterical people.

They were searching for a murderer. They didn't care about her nightmares.

"Alright." She smiled. "Thank you."

"So tell me about this." She unrolls a map out on the floor, using her foot to hold down one end and his foot to hold down the other. It's littered with x's, some spots circled, some with prices next to them. "What is all this?"

"Places I want to have houses in the future."

She rolls her eyes and glances at him. "You want to have a lot of houses in Australia, then."

"Doesn't everyone?" A slight pause, the camera centering on the map so that the points come into focus, and then he zooms back out. "They're places I want to go," he says, and his voice is quiet. Like it's an admission. "A bucket list, of sorts."

"I didn't know you liked to travel," she says, but her eyes are dancing, barely looking at him in favor of studying all the places that are marked. "There are some interesting places on here. You're going to have to tell me the stories behind why you chose them."

"I'll have to remember them all first." He laughs once. "There are a lot." He pauses again, long enough she looks up at him and waits for him to speak, and then says, "So."

"So?"

"...Would you want to go with me on an adventure or two?"
She grins. "When are we not on an adventure?"

Beth said, "I was kind of hoping this would put you off garage sales for at least a couple months."

Meg ignored her and pressed harder on the gas pedal, looking out at the houses as they passed. She wasn't looking for a garage sale, she was looking for *the* garage sale. If the police wouldn't take her seriously, wouldn't tell her anything, then she would find out her own way.

"Seriously," Beth pressed, "Would you say something? Please?"

"I'm driving," Meg said flatly, keeping a lookout as she drove. She had worried that she wouldn't remember the house they had found the tapes at. Instead, the opposite had happened. Everything was as clear as if she had last been here a day ago. Adrenaline, maybe.

"Seriously," Beth repeated. "What are you planning to do? You can't interrogate anyone. You're too short."

It was a funny image, sure, but Meg pursed her lips and didn't reply. She had thought, originally, when Beth agreed to come with her, that they were on the same side. Now she wondered if Beth had only come to keep an eye on her.

When she hadn't said anything for long enough that it stood as an answer, Beth asked softly, "What did you expect?" and it felt like a kick in the throat.

"I don't want to talk about it," Meg snapped, forcing down the humiliated tears that wanted to surface when she thought too long about how everyone was talking about her. She *knew* what she saw. And she needed to know why she had seen it. Why did everyone think that was an unusual response?

"Hey," Beth said, faltering, "I didn't..."

"I don't want to talk about it!"

Beth took a deep breath. "Can you at least pretend to laugh when I try to cheer you up?"

Meg swallowed. "I don't feel like laughing yet." She could see the roof of the house coming up the street, covered in moss and pine needles, and tried to ready herself. Maybe she could get the address of the people who donated the videos, and when she tracked them down the girl would open the door and laugh about how they found their art project. "We're here."

They pulled up on the street, but it took her a second to find the house; it had transformed in the last few weeks. Last time they had been here, everything was open: the windows, the doors, the garage, the patio. Now the house was silent, closed up like a snail retreated into its shell. The curtains were drawn tight, and the flowers drooped and died in the flowerbeds in between dandelions and grass. There were four newspapers in the driveway in place of tables or cars.

"Well, this is a good sign," Beth said with a sigh, stepping through the garden to get to the front door and read the piece of paper taped to it. "Foreclosed. Everything's cleared out." She turned to Meg, her face sympathetic. Just like the officers. "I don't think we're going to get him to tell us who donated those tapes."

"He wasn't paying attention to anything. He probably wouldn't have remembered, anyway." Meg looked at the houses across the street. There were cars in the driveway, but all the curtains were drawn. It was a quiet community, she guessed, that didn't like people sticking their noses into their business. She could knock and ask what happened to the person across the street—she intended to, she didn't know what else to do—but the odds were low that anyone would tell her even if they did know.

A dead end.

They sit on the roof, looking out over the forest instead of the ocean. The faint sound of birdsong carries up to them, the sky stained with pink and orange hues, swirled together like watercolor on canvas. There are a few clouds in the sky, cotton candy

light and puffy, moving lazily in the same direction that the treetops sway just below them.

As they watch, one of the trees close to the edge of the forest bends back the other direction when the wind stops, moving after all of the others have stilled. There is a distant creak, but it doesn't fall.

"It looks like it's going to lose some branches," she whispers.

"If it doesn't come down completely. After dry summers, we get a lot of dead trees."

"That's too bad."

The wind picks up. Another crack, softer, further away, as a flock of birds lifts out of the treetops and flies toward the ocean.

Meg came home from the police station, and for once it wasn't the sting of rejection that made her run for the videos.

It was a spark of recognition.

"What are you hoping to accomplish with this, exactly?" Beth asked. "I think you would have said something if they said their names at any point."

They hadn't—not full names, anyways. For the most part, they didn't need to because they were so familiar, or if they had, she hadn't noticed because it didn't matter. But the officers being tight-lipped had led her to a couple of possibilities as to why, with nicknames and a picture of the girl and a clear shot of the murder happening, there had been no arrests yet.

There was a piece tugging at her memory, and she fast-forwarded through their happiness, which made her feel sick now that she knew how it ended. Misplaced. The girl trusted the wrong person and it cost her.

Stop, she told herself. *You don't want to think about this. You don't want it to be real. You want to forget.*

But she couldn't.

"So..." Beth started. "Your mom called *me* to see why you're not returning her calls. And I think your dad is next. Think that's something you can take care of? You know, before they book a plane out here?"

She was so subtle when she wanted to be. "I'll call her after work..." She paused, doing the math in her head. With the three-hour difference between Washington and Florida, they would be asleep by the time she was finished. Plus, she wasn't sure if she was going in to work tomorrow. "I'll call her back. Promise."

"Right." Beth didn't sound convinced. "So why are you watching it again this time?"

"I've been thinking about this wrong," Meg said, feeling for the first time in weeks like she could laugh with exhilaration. "I thought the police didn't know who they were."

"If they knew who they were, wouldn't they have arrested him?"

"That's what I thought. But..." She paused on a picture of the girl, on one of the days they were down on the beach: the day she got him the dog. Her tennis shoes were blinding white as only brand-new shoes could be, and her jacket was heavy but sleek and stylish, and her hair was magazine-perfect in spite of the wind. "Look at her. She looks like she just stepped out of a catalog."

Beth glanced at her warily. "What are you saying?"

"I'm saying they're both rich." She stood up, running their nicknames through her head—Liz and Cal—and jogged for the computer. She knew what to search for this time. "I should have guessed that from the start. In this video he says 'how did your friend even get in here'—it's a private beach. And it's an old mansion, but it's still a mansion."

Cal + Washington + private beach + death.

The police would have figured this out long before she had, done the same thing she was doing now. If the people in the video were rich, they might have fame. If they had fame, there was a trail on the internet to follow. The officers she showed this to would have known within a day, with their database, who they both were. They knew who to arrest for this.

But as far as she knew—as far as they would tell her—they had done nothing. Because if you had money, you could get out of anything.

Not this time, she thought. If she could just confront them about it, they would have to act. He wouldn't be able to buy his way out of this.

His name wasn't coming up with anything, so she tried the girl's.

Liz + Washington + private beach + death.

And it was her. Smiling brightly at the camera, long blonde hair cut perfectly and swept over one shoulder, presenting her engagement ring to the photographer. As vibrant as if she were alive, as fun-loving as she had been in the videos, but the outline was a wooden frame: a picture of a picture, the kind you saw on an altar or at a funeral service.

Death on private beach shocks community.

"That's her," Meg said, lightheaded with certainty and the feeling of falling into something that, now, completely, was *real*. "Look at the picture. It's her."

"You don't sound happy."

"I didn't *want* to be right." Meg glanced back at the television screen. Same person, same smile, and connecting them felt like digging up a grave. "Okay. Now I just need to look up who her fiancé was and go back to the police."

"They would have found this. What are you going to say?"

"That I know who did it and I want them to do their job," she said, clicking the article. It was from just over a year ago, and she skimmed through it, looking for the name.

Calvin Arud. His name was hyperlinked, which was odd. Meg frowned and clicked it.

Instead of going to a profile like she had expected, the link led her to an actual website. One with professional graphics and a skilled photographer, making it eye-catching and hard to forget.

There was a picture, front and center, of a man with pale skin, slightly-curly brown hair, and a smile so clean and wide it looked photoshopped on, wearing a well-tailored suit with a navy-blue tie. He looked impeccable, and kind, with a smile that you instantly felt you could trust.

Calvin Arud, it said underneath, *Agent: Stella LeRue, contact....*

Meg's hopes dropped.

He was rich *and* he was a professional actor.

This was going to be harder than she had thought.

The officer Meg spoke to this time looked... not quite exasperated, but she definitely didn't look pleased to know the name of a murderer.

"How did you find this?" he asked.

"The girl's picture matches." Meg pointed to the picture she had found. "It was her fiancé who pushed her. It has to be him."

"Allegedly."

Meg stared at him; he didn't so much as blink. He was being serious. "You saw the video."

"We never saw his face."

She had never understood the expression that someone could 'burn,' but she felt it now. This was an *excuse.* "You know it was him!"

"We suspect it was him. But..." He hesitated a moment. "I'm sorry, but it's not that simple. I wasn't part of the original case, but he would have been questioned. Everything matched up, the case was closed. They even made movies together sometimes, so it might even be staged."

Meg wasn't sure whether to laugh or cry. The thought that she had found somebody's audition tape, that none of it was real, was both utterly humiliating and so tempting to accept. "And the way that she died?" she managed.

"It would be a stretch to say it's a coincidence," the man admitted. "But that's not proof. If anything, it seems like someone's trying to frame him. Why would he film himself committing murder?"

"Because people are sick," Meg snapped. "You have to know that." Just from what she had seen, what stories she had heard, what she had *experienced*, she knew that. "All of this just because you can't see his face?"

Beth scoffed and tugged on her arm; she had to consciously work to unclench her hands from the counter when she backed up. "No, because he's rich. Come on. Let's go."

Meg pulled free of her grip and stalked out, her mind spinning. She had known it would be difficult. She hadn't known they would ignore her completely.

That was fine. She would find another way.

Chapter Five

There was an address for Calvin Arud's house, if you dug through maps and connected it to his agent's information: along the Washington coast, just like Meg had suspected.

What she hadn't counted on was that it was only two hours to the west—easy enough to drive to, if she dared.

They might find some memory of the girl there.

There was only one way to know for sure.

Calvin Arud lived on the coast in the north, just past the Olympics but far enough away that the scenery was disconcertingly unfamiliar, and in spite of the distance Meg didn't pay much attention to Beth's attempts at conversation. She couldn't focus on anything except ticking off the miles. Part of it was that she wasn't used to wearing a dress. She and Beth had decided to look nice enough they wouldn't attract too much attention snooping around someone's property, and the dresses worked for that but she was sure she was going to freeze the second they got out of the car. At least they wouldn't be arrested. Probably. Beth didn't look bothered, but Meg felt more like she was a kid playing dress-up.

Plus, in addition to rich and kind-of-famous, Calvin Arud was, probably, a murderer. And the combination of those three things had her clutching the steering wheel so hard that she couldn't feel her knuckles for the whole trip.

Finally, they arrived. Meg turned down a private barely-marked side road leading to the coast, drove through a mile of thick trees that nearly blotted out the light of the sun, and into a clearing with wrought iron fence and a grand house.

It was *the* house.

Meg recognized it, but seeing it in person, she realized the video had done it no justice. It was three stories tall, with dozens of windows and an octagon-shaped turret facing the sea. Although clean and clearly well-cared for, spots betrayed its age: the paint was thin and peeling so that the blue turned to gray, the windows clouded with dirt and time, and rose bushes crept up the sides toward the second story and spread out across the grounds like in the fairy tales she had read as a kid. With the sun low on the horizon it cast a shadow across everything before it, and the wind picked up dry leaves that skittered like spiders across the lawn and into the doorstop.

It was only a short distance away, but it felt further, nearly untouchable. To cross the fence wasn't just to trespass; it was to step back in time, the same odd sense that she had gotten while watching the video. This house belonged in a different century than she did.

"I have to admit," Beth said after a while, making no move to get out of the car, "That looks like the kind of house people get murdered in."

Meg couldn't think of anything reassuring to say. That was probably what she should have done, since this was her idea, but her voice wouldn't work with the magnitude of the truth settling into place. This was *it*. This was the house, where they stood on the green grass and played and laughed as if they would be young and in love forever. This was the sea, where the waves delivered a sandal to a young man who followed it to a young woman and led to their love. This was the cliff, at the end of the lawn plummeting into nothingness.

When she closed her eyes, she was there again.

"So," Beth said, forcing a laugh, "We going to see if he's here or what?"

Meg took a deep breath—*courage,* she needed to know the answer—and opened her door. "Yeah. I'm going to go toward the cliff. You go see if there's a way through the gate."

"Sure, sure, give me the fun one," Beth muttered, but Meg was already out and walking toward the sea.

It was freezing, as she expected, with the wind whipping against her bare legs, and even before she was close to the edge the smell of the salt was so strong it stung. She shivered, running her hands over her arms and grateful she had thought to bring a jacket—but it wasn't just the wind. The way the house stood on the edge of her vision, and the dirt road that they had driven up, and the wild ocean in front of them beginning to churn... She could feel the age in this place. It was ancient. She wasn't just trespassing—she was someplace beyond her comprehension, her feet on hostile soil. A beautiful graveyard.

But she couldn't go back.

Meg stopped at the edge of the cliff. The view was breathtaking, the ocean a panoramic view in front of her. The sky met the horizon and melded seamlessly, the muted blues and greens and grays, and her eyes followed the path of the sun down...

To the rocks, jagged and wide, slick gray stone, the waves reaching toward the ones far beneath her feet as the tide crawled in.

She could see the body on it. Warm but not moving, arms askew, glassy eyes staring up and meeting Meg's as clearly as if she was still breathing...

Something touched her shoulder.

Meg spun around—and the edge of the cliff fell out from beneath her feet.

She didn't have the breath to yell before she stopped in midair, feet on the edge of the grass and heels on nothing, and there was a man holding her by one hand.

Calvin Arud. She knew his face from her research, had been thinking of it ever since she saw his picture and wondered if he was capable of murder, and now he held her hand between her and death and he didn't flinch. He didn't move. His eyes seemed distant and calm, like clear water, as he stared at her, stood still, and thought.

The scream was building in her throat, she was trying to scream, but it died before it made sound so she was only taking heaving shuddering breaths. She was hanging backwards off the cliff, her shoes were slipping, he was just staring at her, please, please be wrong—

(*CRACK.*)

He pulled his hand back, righting her and guiding her away from the cliff, and Meg was so relieved and so short of breath she could have passed out. Might have, maybe, but she thought *Beth* and *the girl* simultaneously and heaved her hands off her knees so she was standing straight. The cliff was still too close, nearly beneath her, and she was dizzyingly aware of it.

Calvin Arud was still standing in front of her, not bothered by the wind or the proximity of the cliff, in a casual gray suit with impeccable trim. Meg watched him carefully, a little sideways, breathing too heavily and too close to snapping, until he took a step back and put his hands in the pockets of his jacket.

"Nasty fall," he said easily.

There was something wrong about him. Something like a snake coiling up in front of her but not showing its fangs yet; the threat was there, waiting, sending her skin crawling with the need to get away. In the past, though, she knew why she didn't feel right about someone, there was a reason. Something in them triggered the distrust—an expression, something they said. From him, though: nothing. He smiled like a normal man she would see on the street.

Maybe that was the problem. He didn't feel like a murderer, but he was too relaxed for nearly watching her die.

"You're Calvin Arud?" she managed.

"I am." His eyes flitted over her shoulder and then back to her face. No expression. Nothing. "I'm really sorry, I didn't mean to startle you. I didn't want you to fall."

"Well, you really helped," Meg ground out. He was at least a head taller than her, and possibly a murderer, and why had she had the bright idea to split up with Beth? Stupid. She should have kept Beth with her, who had all the fury of a mountain lion when backed up against the wall—or edge of a cliff.

His smile widened, and he took another step back; her pulse normalized, just a touch. Now she had room to sprint. To get away from the cliff, and him.

"I really am sorry," he said. "What's your name?"

"...Meg." She felt a prickle of unease at giving her last name, but she didn't see another way. "Meg Schuller. I was hoping to meet you, Mr. Arud."

"Please, call me Cal." He tilted his head. "Is there something I can help you with?"

"No. Well, I mean, yes, of course, I..." Meg took a deep breath and composed herself. "Well, mostly I just wanted to meet you. My friend and I. This was the only way we knew to find you."

Cal raised an eyebrow. It did sound, when she said that, like *she* was the crazy person. She hadn't expected him to be home.

"We've been thinking about acting," she blurted on a whim. "And you're well-established, and live in the area, and we knew where to find you... It seemed like a good idea this morning, I promise."

He laughed and stepped to the side, holding out a hand in invitation to walk in front of him; Meg had a split second to decide what was safer, and decided to walk at his side so she could watch him. "I'm honored you think I'm someone worth visiting," he said as they started in the direction of the fence, away from the cliff. "Have you had any jobs yet? Do you have an agent?"

"No. That's why we came to see you—we haven't had any luck. Well, that and my friend wanted a road trip. We do one every summer." The lies just kept coming. She just kept spinning, because the fewer truths he knew, the less dangerous he felt. "She'll be so excited to meet you. She's wandering around here somewhere—"

His hand landed on her wrist, and she spun around and out of reach; he looked apologetic, and pulled back again. "I'm sorry, but I'm afraid I'm going to have to ask you and your friend to leave. This is a private residence, and I'm here on a schedule."

Meg narrowed her eyes; Cal blinked back at her, looking... normal. Even nicer than she would expect from catching someone trespassing.

But the video.

"Alright," she said carefully, "I'll grab her and we'll leave."

"I would like to meet her before you leave," Cal added as she led the way to the edge of the gated house; Beth had wandered back around and was waving, like they could somehow miss her when her red dress was like a flare on the dull gray of the sky and green of the lawn. "Since you traveled all this way. I just can't make exceptions or I'll have visitors every minute of the day. What's her name?"

"Beth. She's my best friend, and a big fan of yours, so thank you for your time."

Cal smiled and faced forward. There was nothing menacing in the smile. Nothing even the slightest bit off in his eyes. No warning bells, anymore. Maybe she was just rattled from the cliff.

But the shadow of the house fell over her, and that feeling of being watched made her throat tight, her hands shake.

It was a long way down from here.

Chapter Six

"I don't think this is a good idea."

"We should put that on a bumper sticker," Meg said, focusing on the computer screen and trying to tune everything else out. There were a lot of results that came up when she typed 'Calvin Arud' and she didn't want to miss something important. "You don't think anything I do is a good idea anymore. When did I become the fun one?"

Beth made a noise like she was gagging on her own spit and sat down on the edge of the desk; that way, Meg had no choice but to look at her as she peered down. She didn't look mad, but since what was left was the amusement someone got from watching something burn to the ground, it didn't make Meg feel any better. "Your idea of fun is getting concerning. And if I'm saying that, we should probably sign you up for therapy."

"This would go faster if you would help me look."

"That's the thing..." Beth leaned over, putting her hand on the edge of the screen like she was going to shut it, so Meg paused and pulled back so her fingers didn't get smashed when she did. Now Beth looked sympathetic, which was somehow worse. "You can't even tell me what you're looking for anymore."

"You know what I'm looking for! I'm looking for—"

"Something to make the police take you seriously." Beth's eyes were accusing. "You know, you work in an hour."

Meg glanced down at the clock in surprise. When she had last looked, she had four hours. Where did the time go? "I'll just call out."

"You did that yesterday."

"So?" Meg tried to mentally track whether she actually had without showing it. She thought that was last week... No, it was last week, too. Beth just didn't know about that one. "I'll tell them I'm sick."

Beth pursed her lips, but looked at the screen. "What are you finding that's so interesting?"

Everything and nothing.

The girl's name was Eliza Fairbanks. According to the articles, she had been engaged to Cal for just under a month when she died in a terrible slip off the cliff, killing her instantly. He was heartbroken, so much that none of the articles mentioned he was under suspicion. (Although maybe that was because of his money, or history. Or decency.) The pictures of her funeral looked more like the wedding she was supposed to have, as though they already had everything ordered and put it to new use, all white flowers and black dresses and a service held on the beach where they had met. There was a foundation established in her honor by her grieving father, who had passed away shortly after her, leaving no family behind.

So much, so beautiful, and the more Meg found out, instead of giving her closure, it made her even angrier. Everything was wrapped up so neatly, put away in the past, and... and there was something wrong with it, with the neatness of it all. They had taken Eliza and turned her into an ideal, and used that ideal to brighten the world in her absence instead of anything growing darker with her death. It was all wrong. Murder was darkness in a beautiful world, a stain that wouldn't be cleansed without the word she kept thinking of more and more often: justice.

It had been an abstract thing driving her, before, but now she felt it. The beauty wasn't deserved, not if she wasn't taken by a tragic accident but was destroyed with someone else's hands. Maybe he couldn't stand her light any more. Maybe he loved her but not enough. Maybe there was something else at stake.

Whatever there was, she couldn't find it. Or at least, hadn't found it yet.

"Meg," Beth said quietly, "You're getting obsessed. You do this, remember?"

Meg spun in her chair to look at her head-on. "What does that mean?" It was a little offending, that wording. Beth was acting like it was a pattern, when this felt all-new and all-important. "Last I checked I didn't go running after murderers every weekend."

"No, I know, but…" In spite of having started the conversation, Beth looked away from her and out the windows. That was worse, somehow, than the judgement. You looked away from things you couldn't bear to watch, sometimes. "I just mean… Whether this guy is a murderer or not, he's bad news. Are you not getting that vibe?"

"No, I am getting *exactly* that vibe," Meg retorted, turning back to the page of web results. "I don't know what to do with it, is the problem. I can't exactly go back to the police because he makes my skin crawl. That's not a valid reason."

"If you keep poking around, we're going to get a valid reason. And not in a good way."

Meg refused to look at her, because she was never all that great at keeping secrets from Beth. She hadn't told her about the cliff, and Cal nearly letting her go. Part of it was that she didn't have any proof that the hesitation had lasted as long as it felt—with the adrenaline pumping through her, so close to death, it had seemed to stretch into hours before he pulled her back onto solid ground. The second was probably just that: a second. A normal person's reaction to a very unusual circumstance.

Part of it was that she was afraid to acknowledge it before she dove back in. It would scare her off, but if he was that volatile, she needed to do this even more.

"Meg?" Beth asked, which meant she had been quiet for too long.

Meg turned back to the computer. She had work to do.

"Meg, if this is about—"

"Don't!" Meg blurted; she felt Beth freeze behind her, knew that she was as startled as she was. She hadn't even been aware of yelling; it had just happened as a reflex because she knew what the next word out of her mouth was going to be and they *did not* talk about it anymore. Out of respect, out of fear, out of not wanting to dig up a grave when it had taken so much out of them to bury it in the first place.

Meg's hand stole into her pocket, finding the smooth rock there, running her thumb over the indent in its surface. She had worn it down, over the years, and just holding it now, turning it over and over in her palm, rubbing her thumb over the smooth edges, she felt herself center. This had been her first story: the one that told her that she didn't find the stories, the stories found her. The one that didn't have an ending and was never going to have one, no matter where she searched, no matter how she longed for it. She had to make up the story in her head, and it was never good enough. When you lost something essential, the story was never good enough.

But there was a reason she had found those tapes. There had to be.

"It's not," Meg said, letting go of it and turning back to her work. Usually she could brace herself, let it go, make herself forget—but when she was caught off guard, the wound came screaming alive again, like it had happened only yesterday. "It's not. Just... I need to do this, okay?"

Beth swung her legs slightly, thinking it over. She was reading into this, in a way that Meg hadn't known she was afraid of until now. Probably hoping to wait it out, if this was a 'thing she did.' Knowing that she was going to have to give up eventually but she had to realize that on her own. Her faith was touching.

"Okay," Beth said at last, giving her a quick hug. "I have to get to work. Good luck."

Meg swallowed. Maybe there actually *was* faith in that. "Thanks."

Beth let herself out, and there was just Meg and the internet and all it had to tell her about Calvin Arud and Eliza Fairbanks and what had gone tragically wrong.

"You know, eventually, that I have to go home, right?"

He laughs. It's smooth like water. Easy. Genuine in a way that people just aren't. "No you don't. You can just stay here. You know that."

She smiles and tucks her hair behind her ear. "I'm yours, but not enough to skip showering."

"Ah. Next time?"

The smile grows. "Next time maybe I'll just move in."

"Well, where else are you supposed to go?"

"I have an idea."

"You do?" Meg leaned back to look at Beth. That was a welcome sentence. She hadn't found anything over the last few days, again. When Beth didn't elaborate, though, she raised an eyebrow. "What?"

"I want your word first," Beth warned her, setting down her bag and leaning against the table. "Because it's great, because I'm the best, but I want you to promise you'll *keep your head.*"

Meg blinked, hoping Beth couldn't see all the sleep she had lost. If she was phrasing it like that, then it was about Eliza, and she needed whatever Beth had found. "I promise."

"Alright. I don't believe you, but here it is."

She reached into her purse and pulled a piece of paper out with a flourish. Meg recognized it immediately. "The charity auction he has every year?"

"Ah. So you did find it."

"I found it. It just doesn't help me, since tickets are, like, five hundred dollars each and sold out months ago."

"Well..." Beth drew the word out, teasing her, and leaned forward with a catlike grin of satisfaction. "Look at the donors."

Meg took it from her, studying it more closely. The invite itself had logos that the website didn't. A couple of small local stores from his area, some bigger companies from Seattle, a national one that was kind of impressive... and a familiar name. *Betty's Art & Craft Supplies.*

"Seriously?" Meg blurted, staring up at Beth. "Your work sponsors his charity?"

"Seriously," Beth said. "In her defense, it's not really advertised that he's a murderer or something. He buys from her when he needs gifts, so she donates a couple necklaces each year."

It had been strange enough to find out he held galas to support conservation. To hear that he also patronized small, local businesses made even less sense. He had seemed so cold when she met him, and the video—but apparently he could be kind. She gave Beth a baffled look, who just shrugged back at her.

"When you're rich, you can have good taste," Beth said, watching her closely for her reaction. "So what do you think? If I ask her, I bet she'll give me her tickets. That way you can at least talk to him, get some closure."

It was a miracle, a great one, but Meg's stomach turned; she'd have to see him face-to-face again. Even if it was the only way she had anymore, when she remembered the hesitation over the cliff, how Eliza had fallen so fast there wasn't even time to scream, it took real effort to keep herself steady.

But if it was true, then he needed to answer for it. So...

Meg scrambled out of her chair and grabbed her in a tight, fierce hug. "You're the best, you know that?"

Beth gave her a slightly pained smile. "I know. This is going to be my first time at a fancy event, by the way, so you're required to let me know if I do anything embarrassing. We should at least be okay to get through the door, but..."

Meg tried to figure out if she was joking, tried not to get her hopes up and failed. "You're coming?"

"Not every day you get to hang out with famous actors in their creepy old houses." Beth's tone was nonchalant, but her expression serious. "Plus, I need to keep you out of trouble."

"I stay out of trouble!" Meg paused. That didn't sound right, even to her. "Or at least, I did before this."

"There it is."

Meg managed to smile at her. "I thought I was crazy."

"You are," Beth admitted, sitting down across from her. She leaned forward and put her hands in her lap, which reminded Meg of having a come-to-Jesus moment with her mom when she was younger. It looked wrong on Beth, who had bright purple eyeliner and jeans with holes in the knees like when they were teenagers but suddenly looked mature and wise. "But... this means something to you."

It was a carefully-worded statement—one Meg couldn't really answer. It would sound stupid, to say it out loud, but... this had never happened before. There were plenty of sad stories out there, for sure: sold wedding rings and brand-new cribs and photo albums still full of people they wanted no memory of by the end of the day. But there had never been one *like this.* So sudden and unexpected and leaving her with such a gaping sense of loss. The girl had become a friend she had known and intended to keep around for a long time.

She had to see it through.

"If he's a murderer," she said, opting for the simplest truth, "He should be brought to justice. You can't tell me I'm wrong on that."

"No, you're right, but we're not police officers, Meg. We don't have any authority. We don't have any *proof.*"

"So we get some," Meg said, and found herself searching Beth's face for some sign, *any* sign, that she understood. "We get some and we bring it to the police. I'll talk to him at the dinner and try to get him to bring up his fiancée. That's a start, right?"

Beth closed her eyes and pursed her lips, looking down at her hands. Deciding.

"You don't have to come," Meg said, even though she really, really wanted her to.

Beth laughed once, harsh and biting, and raised her head to look at her with affection. "Yeah, I do. You know, at least to make sure you don't get arrested."

Meg swallowed her desperation. The relief, of not being alone, was like air when she had been drowning. "Partner in crime, then?"

"Partners in something, anyway," Beth said with a wry smile. "Now come on. We need fancy dresses."

Chapter Seven

"**S**everely underdressed," Beth whispered, with the tone of voice people used to say someone was flat-lining. "*Severely underdressed.*"

Sad part was, they weren't even in the door yet and Meg had to agree with her. She had thought, when they spent two hundred dollars on dresses and another hundred on jewelry, that they would fit in at least at a glance. No such luck. There were only subtle differences between them and the other guests, but apparently if you had a trained eye they were obvious. They were getting looks already.

Maybe it was their outfits. Meg had never felt such smooth fabric in her life as whatever her dress was made of, close to silk and light as water, but she could tell the others were sleeker, even more elaborate and obscenely clean, and it was a physical distance between them. A stature. She walked by one woman's dress, with so many crystals and tiny beads on it she could see her reflection, and realized it had probably cost a thousand dollars, at least. And the jewelry on some of them would give her a panic attack to pick up in the store, the men wore watches that cost ten thousand dollars, there were Ferraris in the driveway...

It all said the same thing: they didn't belong here.

Beth breathed out through her nose. "Maybe we should have snuck in as a member of the cleaning staff," she said under her breath.

"Just stay focused. We need to find Cal."

"What? So *he* can sneer at us?" Beth moved a tad closer to her. It was unusual for her to be more nervous than Meg, but she could understand it this time.

Meg had opted for a black dress—normal. Beth's dress was bright blue with a crystal-studded belt, so she stood out like a beacon. "You never told me what exactly you planned to do once we got here. Just corner him and question him about—?"

"No," Meg interrupted, and fortunately Beth quieted. They were already attracting too much attention; she didn't want to say the word 'murder' in this crowd. "No. But... I'm going to look around, at least."

"Hm." Beth covertly took a glass of champagne from a tray, most of the way to downing the whole thing before she remembered that wasn't eloquent and lowered it. "Well, I think they're going to notice if you disappear on your own."

"Don't worry, I'll be careful." Meg winked to get her to smile and turned away. She considered picking up her own glass, but decided against it. It wouldn't actually help her courage, no matter how much she wanted it. And she needed a clear head.

That being said, she had no idea where she was going to start looking. She glanced around for anything unusual, anything that seemed dangerous. That was going to be all she had: just a gut feeling that something was off or looked familiar to the videos or reminded her of the girl. *Eliza,* she corrected herself. Her name was Eliza. Using her name made it more tangible, that this was a life that had ended instead of a character in a video. It reminded her of the stakes—made it something real.

She scanned the crowd and the room they were in. It was a beautiful house, she had to admit. It gave her the same feeling as the grand sweeping ceilings of a church, even if the room was only about fifteen feet high. There were actual chandeliers, throwing light into every corner as they slightly moved with the house, and the soft chime of crystal clinking and low orchestra music and murmur of the crowd were soothing, melodic. But there was also something unsettling about the solemnness—a feeling tingling at the base of her spine, like fingers brushing the small of her back, that kept her spinning around and looking for something that didn't belong. It made the soft music feel distant, from another time, as though she was hearing it from behind a wall. *You're not supposed to be here.*

Either way, she wasn't going to find answers in the crowd of people. She needed to keep going—into the dark, in the hallways. They weren't blocked off, there was nobody keeping guests out, but they didn't seem to be calling to anyone else and they were empty.

Which meant she had to go there.

Slowly, as inconspicuously as she could, Meg moved toward the nearest one. The gravity changed when she stepped out of the light and into the dark, the low sounds of the party disappearing into a dim hum. Her footfalls were heavier, louder; though the ceiling was still two feet above her head, it pressed down on her shoulders and shaped her into a crouch. The sudden absence of sound that made her steps echo reminded her more of a tunnel than a hallway.

She turned down the next hallway and froze guiltily: there was a person at the end. A man, with hunched over shoulders like he felt the pressure, too, and tiny wisps of gray-white hair on his scalp, and when she stopped he turned to look at her. His eyes were unfocused in the light, seeing her but also seeing through her, and she found herself frozen in place. It looked like he was waiting for her.

When he didn't say anything, just continued to stare, Meg cleared her throat. "I'm... sorry. I think I'm lost."

He blinked, slowly. "You are."

It was almost a question, but not quite. His voice was very low, slow even though the sentence was short. He held a broom in one hand—it was gnarled, very pale like all the light had been leached out of the skin—but loosely, as an afterthought. A housekeeper, she guessed.

Maybe he knew something about Eliza. The only problem was that she didn't know how to ask.

"It's a beautiful house," she said. "You do a good job taking care of it."

He blinked at her again, and then turned mostly back around and started to sweep. There was a thin layer of dust, even with the event one wall away. "Not much to take care of," he said. "It's not lived in."

Meg frowned. "But doesn't... Cal live here? And his parents?"

"No mother." He shook his head once. "And they don't live here. Only move through."

Move through? He was speaking in riddles. "I'm sorry, I don't follow," Meg said.

He cocked his head in her direction, then went back to moving the broom back and forth. "It's not safe here," he said quietly. "It's safe now, but not later. Don't forget."

Meg caught her breath; he *did* know something. She heard it in both the cryptic answers and the silences. What did he know about Eliza—or about her?

She opened her mouth to ask, but the floor creaked behind her, and she spun around and backed against the wall in the same motion.

Cal stared back at her, silent and unsurprised, and slowly looked her over. When his eyes rested on the jeweled collar on her dress, she had to resist the urge to put a hand over it. It felt fake to be wearing it. It *was* fake.

She glanced back over her shoulder for the housekeeper, for backup, but he wasn't there anymore.

A shiver ran down her spine, and she turned back to Cal with a smile that stretched at every one of her muscles.

I'm not crazy. I'm not crazy.

"Meg, right?" Cal took a few steps forward so they were facing each other comfortably. "It's nice to see you again—although I didn't expect it to be so soon."

Meg shrugged, trying to seem casual even though her heart was hammering. *No witnesses,* the back of her mind whispered to her, *nobody to help you.* "I was around. Is that alright?"

"Of course it is." Cal's eyes darted down, and then back up. There was nothing behind his eyes that she could believe was real. He could shutter out one emotion and seem like a whole new person so fast it gave her whiplash, so the whisper of warmth in his eyes meant nothing. "You look beautiful."

Meg smiled a little but she didn't feel it. Her dress was black and all the way to the floor so that it was hard to walk, and the collar was tight around her throat. It felt kind of like a noose. She was trying not to think about it. "Thanks."

Cal, on the other hand, moved in his suit like he had been born in it. He put his hands in his pockets and leaned against the wall, casual, a king in his castle. "What's wrong? You look worried about something."

Meg schooled her face into careful neutral, and then into a smile. "Not really my crowd," she admitted.

Cal's smile widened for a second before he caught himself. "Forgive me if this is rude, but... then what are you doing here?"

"Beth works for one of your donors, so we were offered tickets. We thought it would be good to see what you do."

Now his eyes were amused. "I'm not in the back hallways."

A veiled accusation. Did he know she was snooping? God she hoped not. She just smiled apologetically. "It's a beautiful house. Sorry, I didn't know the rest of it was off-limits."

"It's not. I'm sorry, I'm just a little protective of it. You understand, I hope." He tilted his head, smiling a little gentler, and took a step so he was at her side. She had to look up to meet his eyes and it made her shrink before she could catch herself. "So. The gala. Is that the real reason you ended up here a week ago?"

"Curiosity is why I ended up here," Meg dared, smiling so he wouldn't take her too seriously. "I didn't get enough when I was here last week, so I thought I'd come back and get a better look. Is that a problem?"

Cal laughed, a normal carefree laugh, and shook his head. "No, of course not. But we should probably hurry back. We're going to miss the auction."

Meg nodded and they wandered back out of the halls, back into the light that was so artificial and bright after the serene dark that it burned at her eyes, and as soon as she caught sight of her Beth made a beeline toward them. Meg braced herself to explain, to play interference, but Cal moved toward another guest and by the time Beth reached her he had been swallowed up by the impeccable crowd.

"You had me worried," Beth whispered, catching her by the arm and discreetly pulling them out of the other guests' sight. "What happened?"

"Nothing. He was just... weird. I ran into a housekeeper who was also weird. That's the theme of the night, I think. Everyone here is just *weird*."

Instead of laughing, Beth looked toward the bulk of the crowd. "Yeah," she said, her tone off. "Speaking of that, take a look at what they're bidding on."

Across the room, Meg barely saw a man at a podium in front of the gathered crowd, a table full of items behind him. Even though she couldn't make out the details, they sparkled and caught the light in so many places they had to have been full diamond necklaces, jewels the size of her palm, keys to a sports car...

But right now, when the participants raised their hands and the amount of money announced went higher, they were looking around the house.

I'm rather protective of this house. It's... special.

Haunted. He meant haunted. She had come across details of that in her internet search but had skimmed over them because they weren't relevant to Cal and Eliza, but apparently at least these people believed it. They were going to stay in the house that Cal and Eliza had lived in, on the edge of the cliff where she had died, but they had no idea what they were really treading on.

"Five thousand!" the man at the podium said. "Five thousand! Do I hear five thousand?" A woman raised her hand, and he pointed at her. "Six thousand! Six thousand for an entire weekend of spooky thrills!"

A man this time.

"Seven thousand! Seven thousand! This is a beautiful house, folks, and you never know what you'll find when the lights go out!"

The woman raised her hand again. One of the men leaned into the other and whispered something, and they both laughed, loud, jubilant, free. No stress from having bid or having lost. They were here for the experience. For the game.

This was it, Meg realized—it was over. There was no way they were going to be able to wrangle the tickets that would get her into the place where Eliza and Cal had lived and the answers were waiting for her. These people were in a whole other league than them.

Instead of defeat, though, the bitterness inside of her felt tangible and solid, a life of its own, a fire stoked by every suspicious glance and person who didn't deign to speak to them and the trust with which Eliza had turned her back.

"Well," Beth said, sounding just as bitter as Meg felt, "This was fun. Remind me to never go on one of your adventures again."

"This one isn't over yet," Meg said, glancing around until she found Cal. He was on the edge of the room, working the crowd, which parted for him like he had a magnetic field. It filled her with such disgust, to see him being accepted by these people so easily. They laughed, smiled, joked, shook his hand, clapped him on the shoulder, everyone around him. Buying the act. Something was *wrong* with him.

And she was going to prove it.

Chapter Eight

This time, Meg didn't tell Beth what she was doing or ask her to come with her. Or even give her any hint of what she was planning. That was how monumentally bad of an idea it was.

She had spent days preparing. Five days. Five days of impatience gnawing at her gut, of lying awake and staring at her dark ceiling instead of sleeping, of preparing and living her routine like she always had. A little easier than usual, actually, because now there was something powering her, pulling her forward like a current in the sea.

Five days of watching the videos, over and over and over, until she knew she was in so deep there was no clawing her way out until it was done.

It wasn't just a video. It wasn't just an act. She knew Eliza like she knew her own thoughts and she wasn't going to leave her lying there on the beach with her murderer looking down. If this was what it took, then so be it.

She had almost gotten out the door unseen when Beth said from the couch, "Wow, you look nice. Where are you going?"

"Thanks." Meg didn't look at her as she picked up her shoes in her hand and unlocked the door. "I'm going out. Be back soon."

"Where?" She stared at her outfit, and Meg hid her shoes behind her back, but she didn't put the pieces together. She hadn't watched the videos as much as Meg had. "Do you have a date?"

Meg turned around, catching a glimpse of herself in the glass as she did. She had curled her hair nicely, pinning it back in a short bun so that it wouldn't get in her face if it was windy. She had gold eyeshadow winged out from her eyes, stark against her skin and sharp on the edge like knives, and she hoped it was reminiscent of golden hair. "I just wanted to get out of the house."

But Beth bit her lip, looking down at her dress, and when she looked back up it was with dawning realization. And anger. "You're going back."

She had been hoping to avoid a fight. "Yeah, but—"

"I thought this was *over*."

"Why would you think that?" Meg demanded. "You know nothing has happened! You know they're still letting him get away with this!"

"Meg," Beth interrupted her. She took a deep breath and put her face in her hands. "Okay. Look…" She started to tick off things on her fingers. Like she was a child. "You're going to a strange man's house. *Alone.* Who has a lot of money. Who lives by himself. Who you think might be a murderer!"

"I…" Meg stopped, avoiding her eyes, still hiding the shoes so Beth couldn't figure out what she was planning to do while she was there. It was… not good. She knew that. But when she opened her phone, looked down at the alert she had set for Cal's name, there was nothing. And there was going to be nothing. Not for months, maybe. Years. She knew how long it took to get people with money prosecuted for small things, much less murder.

She couldn't do this for months. She *refused*.

Beth was still staring at her. It was pleading, now. It made her feel small, and low. "Meg. Come on."

There was a picture on the wall next to the door, so they could see it every time they came home: her, and Beth, and their friend Dinah. Dinah was grinning in the photo, so wide that it was lopsided and full of teeth. Her jacket was covered in cartoon characters and she was wearing a clearly handmade beaded necklace, and it made her look so damn young. So small.

When she faltered, she just had to look at it, feel the anger rising in her chest, and her resolve would return. This time, it gave her the strength to turn her back on Beth. "I'll be careful," she said, opening the door. "If I'm not dead, I'll be back by tonight."

When Beth didn't reply before she shut the door, she had to admit she shouldn't have put it that way. But it was too late.

Story of my life, she thought bitterly, and got into her car barefoot.

The camera focuses out the window of a moving car; the sky is pink with sunrise. There are no other cars on the road, and the camera turns to the interior. She's driving, her hair pulled back in a ponytail, no makeup, wearing sweatpants and an oversized sweatshirt.

She does a double-take when she sees him filming, and then rolls her eyes. "You're going to give yourself motion sickness when you watch this later, you know."

"You just don't want to own up to why we're here."

"We're here because I can't believe you've never been to this beach!"

"I have my own beach. Why would I need to go to another one?"

She rolls her eyes. "The world is a lot bigger than your house, Cal. I can't believe you haven't seen it."

By the time she reached the house, Meg's nerves were so bad she was shaking in her car as she idled outside the gate.

"Stupid," she muttered to herself. "Stupid, stupid, stupid, this is a *stupid* idea. You're going to get arrested in the best case and murdered in the worst. Just drive away. Drive away while you still can."

Saying the words out loud, though, didn't actually change her mind in the slightest; if anything, the idea that she might be going crazy made her all that more violently shut off the car and take a deep breath.

She was not crazy. Not this time. Not about this.

There was a specific thing she wanted to try, though, that admittedly *was* crazy, so she just sat in her car outside the gates, waiting for Cal to come open them. She was gambling that even if there was more than one person here, it would be him who would recognize her car, or her, and come to tell her off in person. She was gambling he would be interested enough to give her a chance to speak.

She was gambling on a lot. Laying it out in a list helped nothing.

After a couple minutes, there was movement in front of her: Cal, just as she had hoped. He was out of his show clothes for the first time, in casual jeans and a t-shirt, walking at a leisurely pace; it didn't make the pressure in her head any lighter. She felt closer to passing out, even, so she ducked out of sight and sucked down one last deep gulp of air.

You can do this. For Eliza.

There was a knock on her window; she jerked her head up and met Cal's gaze, pinning her in place. She had his attention, alright. Now she had to use it.

Meg took a deep breath—she had to do it now or give up—and opened her car door. "Hello again."

Cal blinked at her, with both surprise and suspicion. "Hello, Meg. Can I help you?"

"Not with much." She smiled up at him, and deliberately stepped out of the car, stood up, and shut the door without looking down. "How are you?"

Cal stopped. He had been reaching for her car door to help her shut it, but his hand hung suspended in midair. His gaze fixated on Meg's folded hands.

On the one white sandal in them, which she hadn't put on yet.

"Sorry. Long drive." She kept smiling even though she wanted to swallow because her throat was so dry she was choking on it. She didn't want to invite the idea that she had been spying on him, she just wanted enough to remind him of the past. She wanted to trigger the same memories, so that he would be intrigued enough to talk with her.

Cal still hadn't moved. Didn't even seem to be breathing. When she swung her sandal to her right hand his eyes followed it like it was a magnet, his expression almost pained.

Meg decided she had pushed as far as she could and leaned down to put it on. "I hope I'm not intruding," she said, trying for nonchalant, and straightened back up; his gaze was finally on her face. She tried to look confused. She wasn't supposed to know what she was doing.

She did, though, and her heart thrummed with it. With an odd excitement she had never felt before, breathless and dark.

"No," Cal said finally, quietly. "Of course not. It's... always good to see you."

His gaze rested on the corners of her eyes—on the winged edges, glittering gold. Good. It was meant to catch his attention. To her, it felt like war paint. She hoped it looked like a different kind of war paint to him.

"I know it's been only a few days since we saw each other, but I was hoping we could talk?" she asked, folding her hands again over her white dress.

And for a long moment, where he was at a loss for words, it seemed like she had stepped too close to his fiancée's ghost and he was going to back away and ask her to leave—or step forward and kiss her. She braced herself against the ground, orienting herself toward the car. It was still unlocked. She ran her fingers over the sharp teeth of her keys.

Come on, she willed, *take the bait.*

He blew out a breath that hung in the air between them; it smelled like mint. She could smell it on the wind, too, coming from the garden just behind the iron fence, so that it wasn't inviting, but wild. Old. Something she shouldn't mess with.

"Come walk with me," he said, and his voice came out fast, like it was an impulse to invite her that he was trying to fight. It didn't sound like a choice.

That was fine. If she wanted answers, it really wasn't one.

If Meg had thought it was cold up on the cliff, she took it back now. She wished to God she hadn't been forced to leave her jacket at home to keep up the illusion. Apparently Eliza had been all about appearances, because she had to have been freezing in most of the videos she had watched.

"Are you cold?" Cal asked.

"No. No, I'm fine." She smiled and passed her hands over her arms, looking down to watch where she was walking. Her sandals didn't have much grip compared to Cal's tennis shoes, but so far he was polite, waiting up for her every few steps so he didn't get too far ahead. Some of the places he set his feet were too sure to be anything but following a well-worn path that he knew by memory.

She looked out over the water. It was a gray day, not quite stormy but coming up on it, and she kept watching for boats or something else of the sort heading for land before it hit. No matter how she strained her eyes, though, there were no people out on the water, no signs of civilization at all. The only way down to the beach had been a trail in the side of the cliff, straight down and faded wooden planks nailed into the stone and rickety with age. She was certain on the way down that she was going to slip in her sandals and crack her head open, but Cal had gone down first and told her which steps were most likely to give out beneath her feet.

So at least for now, he seemed to care about the game she was playing. She just had to play it carefully.

"This beach doesn't look like it's been touched in years," she said, just to break the silence.

Cal shrugged, pointing out a rock that would support her without shifting. "It's a private beach—the only way down is on the property, so we don't get a lot of trespassers. And... it doesn't get as much use as it deserves. I love it, but it's kind of treacherous down here, and you need a good day or you spend the whole time watching for the tide to come in."

She hadn't even considered the tide. She glanced up, but it was at least fifteen yards out, and the waves that came in weren't reaching for their feet. They probably had hours left before they would be in any danger.

"It's on the way out right now," Cal said, paused once again, looking at her over his shoulder. Cold sunlight fell around him, so when he smiled it looked rare and different and she didn't know if her shudder was anticipation or fear. "We're fine. I know this beach."

"You grew up here?"

"In bits and pieces, yes. Here and other places."

He waited for her to catch up, slightly behind her now; Meg's skin crawled with the inability to watch him, and it took all her willpower not to turn around.

"It's beautiful," she said instead, looking not at him but at the waves. "Like something out of an old photograph."

She felt his footsteps pause behind her. She had expected it, but she kept walking for a few steps before stopping, as if she hadn't meant to catch him off guard. He was staring at her, but also through her. There was recognition in his eyes, just below the surface, remembering but not sure where from.

Good. She smiled at him, kindly but a little confused, and he shook himself and smiled back at her shakily.

"Yes. I was very lucky to live here." He shrugged and caught up with her again. "Although it doesn't look any different from any of the other beaches. It's just special because it's mine."

"That's incredible." She paused, looking up and down the beach. That explained why there was no dock or boats. "But... it has to connect to a public beach somewhere, right?"

"Not for miles." He smiled a little modestly and held out his hand to help her over a fallen log; even to keep up the illusion that she trusted him she wouldn't accept it, and he moved on without comment. "And it's been in my family for generations. This house, and this beach... They're very important to us. I'd rather be here than anywhere else."

He trailed off like there was more he wanted to say but couldn't. His fiancée had died here, after all, and for a second Meg thought he was going to come right out and say it. But he didn't, and the silence between them was charged. He didn't know what to think about her.

She had to act before that changed.

Meg took a deep breath. Now or never. She had to jump in with both feet and hope he would pull her back up, just this once.

"I was hoping to ask you a favor," she said.

Cal laughed once. "Well, you certainly know how to get to the point."

"It's what I came for," Meg said, stopping so she could face him fully. She didn't look down at the rocks at her feet. She was afraid she'd recognize them and freeze and ruin the whole thing. "If it's not too forward. I never know when I'm asking for too much."

Cal stopped, too, putting his hands in his pockets. "You never know until you try."

"At the dinner," she said. "Those tours of the house... I went with the hopes of getting to bid on one of those. I had no idea they were going to go for that much."

"Those were actually not as expensive as usual." His smile widened, amused, and Meg's smile hurt the corners of her mouth with the effort to keep it in place.

"Yeah, well... I was new to the whole thing, in case you couldn't tell." Meg tilted her head and put her hands behind her back. She had to play a certain role. She had to look doe-eyed and fragile even when she felt ready to burst out of her own skin. She was *so close.* "Is there any way you would be willing to part with one more ticket? Maybe two?"

Cal took a step forward; it took real effort to keep her breathing steady. He had to look down at her he was so much taller, which made his gaze look slanted and sly, but not in a threatening way.

"You're rather obsessed with me," he said lowly. "You and your friend. Should I be concerned?"

Meg took a step forward, too, so that they were close enough to kiss—but kept her lips sealed tight. Eager, but not too eager. The idea of kissing him made her heart pound but not in the right way. In the running from a panther way. In the jumping into shark-infested waters way.

"I don't know you yet," she said—from the video. She had practiced in the car, the exact nuance of the girl's voice, the exact words in her mouth, the exact look in her eyes. "But I think I'd like to. And this place... it feels important to you."

Cal's eyes widened. For the first time since she had met him, he was struck speechless. It was gratifying, but she wondered if she had struck too low. If she had unearthed something she wasn't supposed to.

"I can arrange that," he said at last, and there was anticipation in his smile.

Meg smiled back at him, sweetly, and felt like she had strapped herself into a roller coaster off the edge of a cliff.

It was a victory, but it didn't feel exactly like a win. Just a start into the unknown.

Chapter Nine

"I don't believe it," Beth said, her expression somewhere between furious and awestruck. "I don't believe it. You fucking *maniac*."

Meg held up the slip of paper: a date and time, set a week down the line, with Cal's phone number scrawled at the bottom. "He's expecting two. We're in."

"You are fucking *insane!*" Beth laughed and grabbed the paper from her. "I don't believe it. Do I even want to know what you did to get this?"

"No. No, you really don't." She was trying not to remember it, really, because she was in such a good mood and remembering made her feel wrong somehow. Maybe it was the way he had looked at her, so close she could feel the warmth from his breath, and smiled like it was a game they were playing.

She was going to play a game, yes, but the stakes were a lot higher than he knew. And if he didn't know yet, then when was he going to find out? She intended to use what she had learned, but she wouldn't know the line until she had already stepped over it.

Beth swallowed and held it up. "So," she said in a softer voice, "Are we really doing this?"

Yes, Meg realized, they were. *She* was going to do this. She was going to honor Eliza's ghost in the only way she could.

"So tell me about this." She stops at a rose bush, bright pink flowers and a climbing vine that is taller than her head. "Do you know anything about these? I know you don't take care of them, but…"

"I don't take care of them, no, but I do know about them." He pauses. Thinking. "This one is older than I am. Some of them are older than my parents."

"That's incredible." She carefully places one of the flowers in the palm of her hand without pulling it off the plant and inhales, closing her eyes to draw it in. The rose is wider and flatter than the ones sold in bouquets, a pink the color of lipstick with dark green leaves. "It smells like perfume."

"Much better than new roses," he says. "Not as pretty, but…"

"Maybe not, but I like these better." She hums, running her fingers over the petals. "They're so gorgeous. And you have so many of these…" She spins in a circle, looking around, and when she faces the camera again she looks awestruck. "You live in the best house I've ever seen."

He laughs modestly. "I think so. I'm glad you like it."

"I love it." She softens, walks backwards further into the garden. "I think I'd love to live here."

"I think… we'd love that too."

When Meg and Beth pulled up in front of the iron gate as the sun started to set, driving Meg's ten-year-old car, there were already two other cars in front of Cal's house. The first one was actually a normal car: out of her price range, but not the sport car she had been expecting. They had probably been saving up for this trip for a while, then, or weren't as flashy as some of the people at the banquet had been. The second was a pick-up truck with mud on the tires that was a different color than on Meg's, more down to Earth than she had expected by far. There was no sign of a third car for the third ticket sold.

"Huh," Beth said. "Well, this weekend's not going to be boring."

"Was that a problem? How high is your bar for excitement these days?"

"Shut up, you." Beth froze marginally, then nudged her shoulder. "There's our guy."

Cal was standing outside, in front of the gate, wearing a dark t-shirt and nice jeans that somehow had no mud on the hems in spite of the dirt. They were casual clothes, but with the rain clouds looming over the top of the house, the exterior—and he—looked much darker, more austere and cold.

But when he caught Meg's eye he smiled, so she smiled back and tucked her hair behind her ear.

"If you do that all weekend I'm going to be kicking you a lot," Beth muttered, sounding disgusted.

"Don't blow our cover. Remember, we're fans. We're excited to be here."

"Sure, sure. Let me put my excited face on."

"More convincing," Meg said, pulling in where Cal indicated, through the gates, which he closed behind her car and started to lock. *That's what normal people do,* she told herself. *Nothing to get your adrenaline going. We haven't even started yet.*

Cal walked toward them through the mud, paying it no mind. She tensed her hands on the steering wheel, flashed her teeth at the mirror to make sure they were clean, and put a soft smile on her face.

Just as she had thought, Cal opened Meg's door for her with a smile just as Beth opened her own. "You made it. I was beginning to wonder if you'd reconsidered."

"Of course not. Just taking the scenic route." Meg got out, holding her purse in her hand so she had an excuse for him not to offer his. "We're not backing out. Not with the potential to see ghosts—and your house, without sneaking around."

Behind her, Beth snorted. Cal's smile widened but it still didn't reach his eyes.

"Right," Beth said. "Although I'm not a *huge* believer in ghosts. So I hope your house is enough to impress me."

"I hope so, too." He shrugged in Meg's direction, almost apologetically. "It isn't exactly something you can turn off and on."

"Well, maybe we'll get lucky." She looked over at the cars, still trying to puzzle over who might have owned them. "Are we... not the last ones here? I thought there were three tickets going at the auction."

"Two of the tickets are for a couple," Cal answered, guiding them toward the front door. "Everyone's inside." He dropped his voice a tic. "Please try not to advertise that you're here as my guests. You can imagine they wouldn't be pleased, having bid on them." *And paid a lot of money for them* was the unspoken second half of that statement, and Meg nodded. She didn't want to draw unnecessary attention, anyways.

He led them through the doors, down a hallway Meg hadn't been down before (this house was so huge she was going to spend as much time getting lost as investigating), and into a formal dining room. The table was dark brown wood with curved legs and long enough to seat twelve, but there were only three people, clustered at the same end.

The two sitting on the left had to be the couple. They were about her parents' age, and sat close together but weren't talking to each other. The woman had black hair, curled on the ends so that it seemed to float on her shoulders. Her husband had dark brown hair that Meg could tell turned wavy when it got too long, slicked down with effort and too much hair gel, and his eyes had smile lines around the edges. His wife's didn't.

The man on the other side of the table, however, had a face that had gotten too much sun and a cowboy hat, and he smiled at them widely. "These are your last-minute reservations, I take it?" he asked, and his voice had a twang on the end. He must have brought the pickup truck.

"Yes." Cal held out his hand to them. "Meg, Beth, this is Bill, Kendra, and Jay. Everyone, Meg and Beth. They'll be joining us this weekend."

Kendra nodded to her as they took their places at the table, tightly but polite enough, and glanced at her husband. Jay patted Kendra's hand, like she needed to be reassured about something, which was odd—although she didn't look particularly happy, considering they had bid on the tickets in the first place. Maybe it had been Jay's idea.

"Nice to meet you," Bill said, and tipped the end of his hat. In stark contrast to the muddy truck, he was wearing a dress shirt and slacks, like he expected to go straight from here to a business meeting without stopping. Interesting man.

"Where are you from?" Beth asked, trying to sound casual and not confused like Meg was.

"Oh, I'm all over the place. I chase ghosts, and this was the only place in the area I hadn't been to yet." He grinned at Cal, a little conspiratorially, whose answering smile was more of a polite grimace. "I've been trying to get this trip for years. Got lucky this time."

"We're pleased to have you," Cal said, glancing at Meg. "All of you. It's always an honor to meet people with so much enthusiasm for my house. I didn't realize until I got older how special it was."

Bill leaned forward. "Is there anything in particular we can expect tonight?"

"It really depends." Cal paused, and gave a glance over his head. Meg didn't know what he was looking at—it was a beautiful room, with its high ceilings and the burnished wood trim, but there were no 'ghosts' here—but when he looked back down, it seemed like he had come to a conclusion. "Some nights are more active than others. Some nights are louder. Sometimes it goes for months with nothing at all. I hope it gives you your money's worth, but there's no way to know."

Bill nodded—oddly calm, considering Meg had just heard that they may have just bid thousands of dollars for a three-night stay in an old house. She glanced at Beth and she had the same look on her face, like she was considering storming out.

It was annoying to share the weekend with them, sure, but not dangerous, which was a good thing. If she got in over her head they would need people on their side against Cal, normal people who wouldn't be suspicious of her and

Beth looking around for evidence but would step in if there was danger. She was willing to bet Kendra would be most likely to get suspicious—she was watching them now—but that meant she would watch Cal, too. They all seemed nice enough, didn't seem to be looking through her and give her the shivers like he did.

And she had Beth, and Beth had her. They would be fine.

"So is it just us?" Meg asked, hoping for casual, she wasn't really going to get a better opening than this. "Is there anyone else here?"

"Mostly just us and my father." Cal shrugged, all false modesty. "We don't get a lot of visitors here."

"I'd guess the gate would do that pretty well," Jay said. "What year is that from?"

"From the early nineteen hundreds." Cal looked up as one of the doors opened, and smiled slightly. "My father could tell you more about that, though. He's our resident history expert."

Even if he hadn't introduced him as his father, Meg would have guessed who he was. Steven Arud and Cal walked with the same sort of confidence, although his father had an odd gait that suggested he had a permanent limp he was trying to downplay. He was in a suit that she knew had been carefully tailored: it made his shoulders look strong, and his neck long, and his torso lean and wiry. She had a feeling without it, he would look very similar to her own father, to anyone else's. He wasn't trying to look like someone's father right now, though; he was trying to look like the owner of a beautiful artifact showing it off and charging for the privilege, the kind of man who knew what he was doing with every step.

And his eyes were Cal's. It was uncanny how much of him looked back at Meg when they lingered on her—the same shifting energy, unreadable, like he had more secrets than truths in his soul.

Mr. Arud stood at the head of the table, and silence fell over them all like a wave; he smiled at them, trying to put them at ease, but Meg's mind recoiled from it instinctively. It looked condescending, and very practiced.

"I can definitely help answer any questions you have about the house's history, but they're going to have to be later. You're going to want to get some sleep. If anything is going to happen…" He stopped for a breath, so that the *if* hung in the air for emphasis. "It's going to be well after sundown."

Beth groaned next to her under her breath, but in the attentive silence it carried. Cal chuckled under his breath and the edges of Mr. Arud's smile quirked.

"I don't pick when the house comes alive," he said. "And I can answer questions, but they're best directed to Cal. He's going to be the one actually giving you the tour."

Beth nudged her under the table and Meg barely nodded to show she heard it. The tour, which had at first seemed like a distraction, now seemed like their best source of information. Cal would be giving the tour, telling the stories, and the stories would reveal the secrets tucked in its corners like cobwebs. There were stains that couldn't be scrubbed out; there were holes in the stories that couldn't be mended with time. She would find them.

Next to her, Beth raised her hand slightly. "You had us sign waivers," she said, voice shaking just a little. Just enough that Meg couldn't tell if she was acting. "Is the house dangerous?"

Bill slightly shook his head like he was amused by her question. "It all depends on what the spirits want, and on how much you respect them." He leaned back in his chair; it seemed he liked holding everyone's attention. "Some healthy respect never hurt anyone. As long as you remember that, you should be fine."

Beth sat up straighter. Meg could see the words building on her tongue, *I'm not scared,* but she held her arm under the table so she swallowed them. Cal was watching them, his eyes intent on Meg in particular, and when Meg looked at him she hoped she looked passive. Let him think she was naïve, a little scared but not enough to be easy prey. Let him think they were here on a coincidence and nothing more. She was afraid of nothing with Beth by her side, holding her hand back in solidarity. She was here for justice, and he was bound by the presence of everyone else here. He couldn't murder her with five witnesses. He couldn't even touch her.

He smiled at her, now. "You're perfectly safe," he said. "They're just precautions. Nothing is going to happen."

Meg gave him her prettiest smile back, full of belief, and nodded that she understood.

Chapter Ten

Meg didn't sleep.

She just couldn't get her brain to shut off. Not in a strange house, full of strange people she didn't know or trust, and especially not when she was by herself. She and Beth had been hoping to room with each other, just to know the other was within reach, but the house wasn't small enough to require that. Cal had offered them rooms at the end of the hall, separated only by a thin wall, and it would be pushing it to suggest she didn't feel safe in his house. So they had agreed.

But now she kind of regretted it. Because half the time it was so silent she wasn't sure *she* was breathing, and the other half she thought she heard someone else breathing. Her mind was inventing things to scare her. That was all.

It wasn't helpful.

She looked down at her phone—no service, same as when she had checked the last three times, but it was just habit to look at it—and the time stared back at her: *1:25.* Fantastic. She was supposed to be asleep and waking back up in less than half an hour, not still lying here staring at the ceiling.

Meg groaned and gave up, put her phone in her pocket, and got out of bed. She wouldn't change out of her PJs, which were just pants and a sweatshirt, so if somebody found her she could say she forgot where the bathroom was. More than likely, though, she was going to be the only one up.

She wasn't sure what she expected to find—it wasn't like she was going to stumble into a room and find something the police had missed—but maybe she could find something. This house was certainly big enough to hold all the secrets of an old family. How was she supposed to find something convincing with so many places for it to hide?

She opened the door and slipped outside into the hallway. It was completely black, a tiny bit of light coming from a window on the far end that had to be moonlight, but when she turned on her cell phone to use as a flashlight she had to shut her eyes before she blinded herself; she quickly turned it back off. She was going to wake everybody else in the house up if she did that, and then her search wouldn't even happen.

Meg took a step forward, just to test; the entire hallway creaked in response, the board protesting all the way up, and she cringed. She waited a second, sure it was ringing through everyone else's rooms, but no doors opened. Nothing broke. Someone coughed, down the hallway, but it sounded random, like they were still asleep.

She put more weight down. Again it creaked, but softer, so she took another step. It was just her racing mind amplifying things, her sureness that she was doing something wrong resurfacing with a vengeance. The noises were loud in her ears, but in the rooms they would be drowned out by the wind and the tree branches rustling and the waves crashing on the beach.

She couldn't believe how old this house *felt*. Like it was sentient, and if not watching then at least watchful. There was a faint hum of electricity, in the background, but it was odd how far off everything else was that she had grown used to. No cars. No people on the sidewalk. No sirens. No planes. They were in their own bubble, in time or on the surface of the moon. She hadn't known a place could feel alive and dead at once, but this did. This was probably how people felt in the jungle before they had weapons: small, a visitor in their own home, a prisoner of their own awareness.

Another step. Her steps didn't just creak, they echoed. She listened again, for Beth to get up since she was in the room right next to her, but nothing.

Slowly, carefully, she moved down the hallway. There was nothing else alive in the house, it seemed. Just her.

Meg breathed out—too loud in the silence—and picked a random room that wouldn't be occupied, opening the door an inch, then two. She expected it to creak, just like the floor did, but the hinges were silent, well-maintained. It was the only sign she had that the house was cared for. Much of it felt abandoned, even with people inside.

She stepped through, waited to see if anything moved, and when she was sure she was alone she eased the door shut and turned on her cell phone, lowering the brightness down to nothing so that her eyes didn't burn. She could at least use the light to look around.

The room was full of furniture, covered with sheets and blankets of varying colors, most of them white. Or at least, they used to be white. Age had grayed them, or maybe the dust. She had the impression, so far, that only the rooms they were in and the ground floor were used; the rest was, by unspoken agreement, roped off and unused and untouched. She understood. It was far too big of a house for three people. She could have fit twenty people comfortably into these rooms—although, she had to admit, it wouldn't help the feeling even if the whole thing was lit. It was just too old. Too watchful.

But then, if there were only three people living here, she didn't know why all of this furniture was here. Maybe it was from before Cal, or even before his father. The legs that she saw peeking from underneath the coverings were intricately carved wood, varnished a dark brown that was almost black, and impeccable underneath the dust like they had never been used.

There was a painted portrait on the wall of a man and woman, three children standing between them. Their clothing was austere and old-fashioned, but even without that she would have known they were Cal's great-grandparents. Somehow, impossibly, they had the same gaze as him. Distant and knowing.

"So how old is your house?" she asks. "Do you know anything about when it was built?"

"It's over a hundred years old. But you know, the story isn't in how it was built..." He lowers his voice for show. She leans closer to the camera attentively. "It's in how it was destroyed."

"Destroyed?" She frowns, looking over her shoulder at it in the distance. "So this isn't the original house that your great-grandparents built?"

"Most of it is. But it had to be restored." He pauses, taking a deep breath, as though immersing himself in this story hurts. "The first time they built it, it was their dream house, my great-grandparents. They worked for years and years, my great-grandfather building it and my great-grandmother raising the children in the unfinished rooms. They poured everything they had into making it the best house anyone had ever seen."

A pause. She nods. "It is a beautiful house. They succeeded."

"Flatterer." The fondness in his voice is clear, gentle. It makes her smile. Another faltering breath. "But in between building it, they began to drift away from each other. They loved each other, but it had lessened, and they both knew it. By the time the house was finished, they barely spoke. They had the house of their dreams, but they didn't have what they had wanted, anymore."

"So in the end, he decided that they couldn't have the life they had hoped for. He told his wife that they didn't need to live here together, that they needed to move on. He decided to leave all of his hard work to her and their children. But she couldn't take it. He wasn't cutting her free; he was leaving her alone. So she asked him for one last dinner together, just the two of them. When he came into the dining room, he found she had doused the entire house in lantern oil."

"So he couldn't leave her, she set them and their house ablaze. Neither of them made it out. Their children, out playing in the low tide, were all that were left of the beautiful life they were going to live together."

It had seemed like a fanciful tale. Looking at them, she could see the air of tragedy coming, and it made her shudder and turn away.

But there was nothing of Eliza or Cal, so she shut off the light from her phone and stepped back outside into the hallway. It creaked under her feet, just enough to set her on edge but not enough to wake anyone up, and she glanced around for a new room to look in. The doors all looked identical, so she crept towards one that she guessed was a closet and stopped.

And a floorboard creaked behind her.

A shiver swept down her spine; she didn't have the courage to turn around. There was nothing there, nobody else was up, she would have heard a door open... and yet she thought she could feel something lingering. Standing, watching her.

Just Cal, she thought, and even though it set her teeth on edge she would take it. He wasn't going to murder her outside his guests' rooms. *He's just standing there to scare you, just like at the cliff. Nothing you can't handle.*

Meg whipped around, and there was nothing there but she heard the floor creak again: with somebody moving away from her, even though there was nowhere to go. There was no actual movement for her eyes to catch but she felt it, a sense she hadn't known she had waking up.

Her skin started to prickle, like bugs were crawling all over her body. There had been someone there, she was so sure, she had heard it behind her...

Just your imagination, she told herself, but it took real effort to face forward. It didn't feel like nothing was there, even though she had just seen the empty hallway. She *knew* it.

Just the house. Although that wasn't comforting either. *Just your nerves. Nothing that can hurt you.*

New room. She needed to get out of this hallway, now. She spun into the nearest room (not her own, although she would have taken it at this point) and closed the door behind her. She strained her ears, but there was no sound behind her this time. No footsteps. No breathing. No floorboards creaking.

She let out her breath and let her head fall against the door. "You're losing it," she whispered to herself. "You're fine, you're fine. Okay..."

She straightened, turned on her phone flashlight—and choked on a scream.

The groundskeeper stood in front of her: his skin was pale white, hair gray-ish-white, clothes gray, and yet she somehow hadn't seen him in the dark. He stared through her, perfectly calm, perfectly still, no apology for startling her or shock on his face to find her snooping around in the dark.

"I..." Meg composed herself and backed against the door all the way so nothing else could sneak up on her. "I'm sorry, you—you—" She swallowed, waiting for him to say something, but he just kept staring. "I... didn't know anyone was in here. I'm sorry."

He tilted his head just a little, to show he was listening. It was oddly catlike. "You shouldn't be here," he said in a thick rasp.

"I didn't know this room was off limits. I'm sorry. I was just looking for the bathroom."

He looked down, away from her, and picked up the sheet off one of the couches before settling it back down. It was a meaningless motion, but practiced, and when he was done he moved to a back bookcase and did the same thing. When Meg looked closer through the dim light from her phone, she could see that it lifted dust off of the sheet and into the air, and then when he moved it swept off with him and onto the floor. There was a broom in the corner that he would use when he was done. It seemed an ineffective way to dust.

"How long have you worked here?" she asked.

He paused—counting the years.

"Since Cal was born?" Meg asked.

"Before," he answered finally. "Many years before."

Wow. She couldn't imagine living in here for years, wandering around in the dark. Only hours here and she was sure the walls were listening to her, every sheet was hiding someone ready to grab her, and the silence was driving her crazy. They were so close to the ocean and the forest but with the door shut she couldn't hear the outside world at all.

"You said before that the house was safe sometimes," Meg ventured. "What did you mean by that?"

Nothing. Secrets he wouldn't part with. This felt like talking to a child: slowly, trying different phrasing to see what got results, hoping for answers but expecting silence.

"Is it safe now?" she tried.

He turned to face her fully at last, setting the broom against the table behind him and not watching to see where it fell from his fingers. His gaze was unsettling, and slippery, moving around her even though his eyes held steady. On a whim, Meg moved her hand up next to her head; the gaze didn't move. He didn't even blink.

He was blind. His gaze was clear, not clouded like she would have expected from his age—but looking closer, she realized the skin around his eyes, where most people had some wrinkles from smiling or frowning, were much more deeply entrenched. Like something had taken away his sight. Something other than time.

If she got closer, she might get a clue. Maybe it was in one of the stories about the house... But this was one mystery that she wasn't sure she could get the answers to and stay here.

"It's not safe," he said, calmly, clearly, "Not with her here."

Her?

Meg spun around to look over her shoulder, even though she was backed against the door and he was blind. There was no one there. Of course there wasn't, and yet... "Who?" she asked.

"Her," he repeated, like he wasn't talking crazy, and his eyes were still fixed over her shoulder like he could see something she couldn't. He was blind. He couldn't. "You should go."

Meg swallowed, hard. She didn't dare take her eyes off of the servant or the darkness around him, so her hand groped blindly in the dark behind her until she found the handle and darted back outside.

She backed up, out into the hallway, and that feeling hit her again, like a sledgehammer, right in her chest: *someone is there.*

She spun around, coming face to face with Cal.

Meg yelped, putting a hand to her heart just to feel the blood rushing there. Just to be sure she wasn't having a heart attack. "I swear to God, Cal."

"Sorry." But he was smiling. Slightly apologetic, slightly amused that his house scared her so much. "If it helps, you startled me just as much. I thought I was the only one up."

"I..." *Was talking to your groundskeeper.* But a quick glance inside the still-open door told her she was alone except for Cal's sudden appearance. There were no other hallways, but the man was gone. Was she going crazy? She pursed her dry lips to keep from shuddering. "I doubt that. And I couldn't sleep. It's so quiet here."

Cal tilted his head, listening for a beat, like he hadn't noticed how silent it was. "That's because it's a calm night. There's a storm blowing in—it won't be quiet then. When the wind picks up, it shakes everything. When I was young I thought a giant was trying to turn the house upside down."

"I can't picture you young," Meg said, but when he looked at her funny she regretted it. That wasn't what people said. She meant it because she knew things about him she wasn't supposed to. When adults were warped, and cruel, you couldn't think of a time they couldn't hurt anyone.

"Well," he said when she didn't explain herself, "Believe it or not, I was. And I thought everything in this house was out to get me. It drove my parents crazy."

That seemed like the sort of thing to smile at, so Meg did, but she was just relieved that comment hadn't caught her in her lie. She had a specific image to portray, and every step away from that was a major risk. To getting kicked out of the house at the least, her and Beth hurt at the worst. She couldn't risk it. The stakes were too high.

"I can see that," she admitted. "It's like nothing I've ever seen, that's for sure. You were so lucky to grow up here, where it's so interesting. All my house does is leak when it rains too much."

Cal's smile widened, and he looked down at his watch. "Well, I hope you got at least some sleep, because we have a long night ahead of us. It's time to get everyone else up. Are you ready for an adventure?"

Meg smiled wider. "When aren't we on an adventure?"

Cal blinked a second, then his smile turned softer, more genuine. "When indeed. Come on. You should get Beth up. She strikes me as the type you should approach with caution."

He moved away a little faster than usual—jarred by her use of a line from the video. By the echo of his dead fiancée Meg kept ringing. She would have to be careful not to overstep it.

...Only, she realized as soon as his back was turned, she hadn't thought about using the video that time. The words had just appeared in her mind and come out of her mouth without pause, without decision, as natural as anything.

Chapter Eleven

There's a logical explanation for everything.

Meg just kept repeating that, walking in line with the others as they went to go look for haunted activity, two paces behind a murderer. Logical. Reasonable. People could be crazy and dangerous without ghosts. Lots of people were. It wasn't comforting, as far as thoughts went, but it kept her eyes forward and not twisting to watch every shadow.

There were especially no ghosts. There. Were. No. Ghosts.

(How was this her life?)

It was just Bill's nervous energy, she suspected. He was the one in front of her in their single-file line, and even though he wasn't speaking, his excitement was tangible. His head kept swiveling from left to right, right to left in the dark, so much she was glad he had left his hat in the room because otherwise he was going to hit her in the face with the rim of it. All the lights were off—Cal was leading them blind, navigating the darkness without so much as a stumble—and it made it a lot easier to imagine the shadows were alive and reaching for her.

It was just one slip-up, because the stories about the house were still in her head and now, standing here, they felt possible. She had watched the videos over and over again. The only way she was going to make it was if she lived and breathed the pieces of Eliza that she had to use.

But with every glance Cal gave her over his shoulder, face hidden so she could only imagine what was in his eyes, she had to fight the dread rising up her throat.

Don't play with things that you can't control, the description of the house had said, and it was just attention-grabbing nonsense but it felt like more.

Behind her, Beth's footsteps were calm and measured, and Kendra and Jay brought up the rear. They still didn't seem as excited to get this tour as Bill was, which Meg didn't understand. They had bid just as much to get this trip as he had—twice as much, even, since they were here together. But she hadn't seen Kendra crack a smile once, and they weren't talking together and hadn't since dinner. Jay was quicker to talk than Kendra, so maybe the trip was his idea and she was humoring him. That seemed like a married couple thing to do.

"So where are we going?" Bill asked. His voice was hushed, but still carried in the silence, and he swallowed; when he spoke again it was even softer. More reverent. "Where is it most active?"

"It depends," Cal answered softly. He had no problems with his volume; Meg understood. If she lived in a house like this, she would learn exactly how loudly to speak and not raise her voice either. It was just enough that they could hear him but no one else could, and he flicked on a flashlight once even the light from the windows didn't illuminate the way. "Right now, on a hunch, we're going to try the basement."

He used the flashlight beam to lead them through a nondescript wooden door and down an even less stable set of stairs; every step squeaked under Meg's footsteps, every sound ricocheting around in her skull. When there was no background noise, when everything was happening in a vacuum, all the sounds inside seemed so much more important, a precursor to danger. She was trying to track everything and it was wearing on her nerves. What would it be like to actually live inside of it?

"Shut the door after you, please, Jay," Cal said, using the flashlight to point at the stairs so people knew where they ended.

He did, and when they reached the bottom of the stairs Cal flicked off the light. Meg felt silly for holding her breath until she realized that the silence meant everyone else was, too.

Something moved behind them, and Beth screamed shortly and grabbed Meg's arm in a vice grip; she was too startled to move at all. One person in the group laughed, a little breathy, but it was like they were holding in a scream too.

Cal turned the flashlight back on, dim enough it wouldn't burn their eyes, and directed it into the corner where the sound had come from. There was something there, for real this time, something that hopped into the light and turned its head to look at them.

A crow, big and jet black, and its beady eyes stared at them and the flashlight without blinking. It wasn't afraid of them, didn't seem threatened by them, and Meg felt like it was looking at her in particular when it cocked its head to face them fully.

"He stays here sometimes," Cal said softly. "We think there's a hole to the outside he can get through, but we've never found it. He doesn't cause any trouble, so we don't chase him out. He's been coming for years."

Meg breathed out shortly; it didn't help ease the dizziness. There were no windows in the basement, only the one door they had used which had been closed and was closed now. Where had it come from?

"That's not right," Beth whispered into Meg's ear fiercely. Meg agreed. It *wasn't* right. When Cal turned the flashlight back off it was so dark that the pitch black swallowed it back up; just like that, they were alone again. She couldn't even hear it anymore, didn't know if it was moving or where it was going or where it had come from, but she felt its eyes, watching her.

Are there other crows or animals down here? She wanted to ask, but she had no breath left in her lungs and it didn't come out at all. She felt eyes. She was piercingly aware that if the crow was two feet in front of her and she couldn't see it for the darkness that there could be other things down here. And she felt them, too.

It was whether they were real or not that was the question.

Don't ask questions you don't want to know the answer to.

They stood in silence; Meg wasn't sure when, exactly, she had backed up, but now she was standing against Kendra and Beth's shoulders on either side of her so that they were a small ring of people. A united front against the dark.

Just against the dark. There was nothing there to fear. Nothing that could hurt her.

And yet. When she breathed, there was something in the air, something different about it. Old. Real. Worn at the edges. Touched by the wildness of the sea. That was what the dark was: alive. Layered.

Wrong.

There was something wrong here. Something deadly. She felt it. She breathed it. *Wrong.* Like a deer smelling a wolf on the wind, and she was the deer. Whatever predator she felt here, its fangs were bigger than hers. The realization had every nerve in her body locked up so that she felt frozen, frozen and on fire all at once, every dangerous memory she had ever had surfacing at the same time. Something was here. Something was—

Behind her.

She spun around, knocking into Kendra in her haste, who hissed out through her teeth in annoyance but didn't say anything. They were in a circle. There was nothing behind her.

Her heart climbed up, up, up her throat; she turned back around, looking for what was wrong, what was down here. Her range of sight was limited with the dark, but it was adjusting and there was nothing there. Nothing to see. Nothing close enough to hurt her. Only the outlines of the furniture and the sheets on them and the boxes at their base and—

A sandal.

The white sandal was in the corner, covered with dust, nearly forgotten, its white flower fraying and melting into the dust it lay in.

Meg couldn't breathe. She pressed her lips together, sealed them. She couldn't scream. She couldn't give away what she saw, because then it would disappear, because then she would seem like the crazy one. The rest of them didn't know the significance of a sandal. They wouldn't know why seeing it felt like stumbling across a tombstone. She was here, seeing that. Eliza was—

A breath of cold air hit the back of her neck; she felt the echo of someone behind her again, but this time she didn't turn around. She didn't dare.

I'm not crazy. I'm not crazy. I'm not crazy.

Beth touched her hand, and she gasped in surprise and spun around to face her; Beth's face was concerned, but not afraid. She hadn't seen the sandal, had only seen Meg freeze, and she mouthed *are you okay?*

Meg shook her head no and squeezed her hand hard enough one of her knuckles cracked. Beth didn't pull away or question it, just quietly let her. She couldn't believe she was going to do this on her own. She was so grateful she and Beth were the same brand of stubborn.

Bill laughed once, a gasp. "I felt that," he said, and this time Meg couldn't find it in her heart to think he was overly zealous. "I *felt* that. Oh my god. Whatever's in here is *strong.*"

Whatever's in here is still in here.

"Nothing happened," Kendra said. Her tone could have meant either she hadn't felt it or denied that she had.

"No," Cal agreed, but his voice was tight. Nervous. He *knew* the house, slept every night with this energy as a blanket over his head, and he was still nervous. "But we should probably go back upstairs."

Nobody argued.

Meg shook the whole way up the stairs, didn't let go of Beth even after they were upstairs again and into places where she didn't feel the dark so pressing on her skin. She was aware that Kendra, at least, was staring at her, but she couldn't bring herself to care.

There had been something down there, but not what they thought. The first proof she had that Eliza had existed at all outside of the video, and it was down there in that basement. It was so fitting.

"Where are we going next?" Bill asked, in a tone of voice like a kid at a candy store. It ground against her nerves, with how much she still had to fight down the urge to shiver.

"I don't know," Cal said, voice still quiet, still perfectly suited for the silence of the house. They were passing through the main ballroom that they had been in for the auction, but with all of the tables pushed off to the side it seemed much larger, and their footsteps that much louder on the hardwood floor. "I'm just following a hunch, but if it was strong there, this is the other place it might be."

That was the last thing Meg wanted, but she had a show to put on, still, so when he glanced back at her she put on a shaky smile and found enough solid ground to let go of Beth's hand. She cast her a concerned glance, but didn't say anything, and Meg hoped she hadn't needed her hand too.

"Through here," Cal said, his voice normalizing a bit, sounding a bit more like a guide than someone being caught off guard by their own house. "This is one of the places where, when I was younger—"

"How much younger?" Bill interrupted, pushing between Meg and Kendra to go stand next to Cal; Meg bumped into Beth a step or two away, who shook her head in exasperation.

Above them, the ceiling creaked, and a shriek rang out that hit right between her eyes—but she knew that sound, from a car crash. It was metal ripping from metal.

And it was *right* above her.

Meg threw herself sideways blindly, hit the floor, just as the glass shattered against the ground, a thousand panes at once. She squeezed her eyes shut against the tiny shards that hit her face, like being on a beach in the windstorm, a million cuts at once.

Next to her, someone started screaming and didn't stop.

Meg forced her eyes open, and it took a second to see past the twisted form in front of her. One of the beautiful chandeliers had fallen from the ceiling above them, and the delicate metal arms were bent the wrong way and snapped away from the base, so tangled with the chains it looked like a deer's antlers caught in a net. All of the tiny pieces of glass, meant to catch the light and refract it, were shattered across the hardwood floor, barely visible in the dark.

Kendra was screaming. There was so much blood on the side of her face that for a terrified second Meg thought it was all torn off, that it would be clinging onto the veins like a peeling mask. It clung to her hands, bright sticky gloves, glowing with the dim light from the window.

"Get towels!" Jay ordered, "Lots of them! Now!"

It was her he was yelling at, Meg recognized that, but she couldn't move. She was stuck in place on the floor. If she moved too much the blood from Kendra's face would coat to her hands and never come off.

"Don't move," Beth whispered, and took off past her at a dead sprint.

"Ha," she replied weakly, but Beth was already gone. She had the first thought of *why* but she was afraid of the answer.

"Is it your eye?" Cal asked, crouched in front of Kendra, and he reached to pull her hand away but she flinched away from him and Jay lunged between them; he retreated fast, no change in his face. "Is it your eye? Can you open your eyes?"

For a second Kendra didn't move, and Meg's stomach flipped with sick anticipation, but after a long pause she breathed out. "No. I can see—barely. It's hard to open it."

Jay moved her hand away, and Meg shut her eyes but not before she caught sight of the hand that came away, coated so completely it looked like she was wearing one red glove. "It doesn't look bad," he murmured; Meg wasn't meant to hear, but she couldn't stop listening, and morbid curiosity made her look again. "You'll need stitches, but you can open your eyes and it doesn't look like it cut through the eyelid." He kissed her forehead, holding her face in his hands. "You'll just have a badass scar."

Kendra said something Meg couldn't make out, and Meg's stomach turned again. So much blood. She was so dizzy it felt like motion sickness. The room was spinning. Or she was. She opened her mouth, trying to suck down more oxygen, but it didn't make her any less nauseous.

"Meg," Cal called, "Are you okay? Are you hurt?"

All she could do was shake her head. She wasn't hurt. Just frozen. Just seeing the bloody shards of crystal, one long enough to be a knife, lying on the ground around her like a map.

"Towels," Beth said, her footsteps pounding on the floor next to Meg's hands. "Here. Use these."

A hand settled on Meg's shoulder; it felt grounding, something to make the spinning a little less tumultuous, and her vision focused. Maybe she should have seen her reflection, but in the dark it just looked like shards of fallen light between her fingers.

Her fingers. She moved them experimentally, just a twitch, and it was like a million fire ants biting into her palms and under her nails and in the folds of her wrists all at once, nothing one at a time but bad enough she cried out when it all hit at once.

"You're hurt," Cal breathed, close enough to her she felt it on her face. She wanted to flinch away from him, but instead everything locked up and turned off. Even through her jacket she felt his hands, on her shoulders, holding her up.

It was very hard to breathe.

"You!" Beth barked. "Back the fuck away from her!" And then she took his place at Meg's shoulder. Her touch was much lighter, and familiar, but shaking. "I told you not to move."

"...Didn't think about it," Meg admitted, keeping her voice and breathing tight so she didn't move her hands at all. She didn't know how she didn't notice it before, now that she was aware of it in every nerve ending. "Didn't realize how close it was."

"Well maybe next time you'll listen to me." Beth moved so she was in front of her, knees not quite touching the floor. "I don't see any blood. I think you're just going to have to lift them straight up so nothing digs in."

Meg nodded, but it took a second more before she could actually rock back onto her knees and get her hands off the ground. They glittered with broken glass shards, tiny dots of glitter she could barely see in the dark.

Beth took her hands to look at them. "Good. That's not bad. And nothing got in your eyes, right?"

"No." She stared at Beth. She was so quiet, so calm. Sure, she always took blows a little easier and stayed on her feet after, but it looked like she was holding it together. Not barely, like her, but completely. "Why are you so calm?"

Beth offered a slim smile and started to clean the glass off. "I'm not."

At least she wasn't screaming. Meg glanced up. Kendra was on her feet, both hands over her eye protectively, Jay supporting her and murmuring things to her with each step and Bill running ahead to open the door without a word. Cal trailed behind both of them, a bloody towel in his hand, staring up at the ceiling where the chandelier had fallen from with a frown. He was only about three feet away from her.

Kendra had been only three feet away from her. It would've been less, but Bill had cut in front of her to get to the door first and she had stumbled.

That was it. That was all that was between beads of blood on her fingers and a sliced open eye. Or forehead. Or skull.

"Hey," Beth said, "Don't think about it."

Which meant she was thinking about it, too. Meg shook herself. "I know. I'm fine."

Beth gave her a look that said she didn't believe her, then went back to clearing off her hands in silence. There was blood on her fingers, and it was drying and coarse against Meg's skin.

From behind the wall where the others had gone, there was one short, shrill cry that made Beth jump and accidentally yank her hand—Kendra, probably, definitely, she had to reassure herself a few times before she could focus on what they were doing again. Head wounds bled a lot. She remembered reading that somewhere once. It was going to be fine because it wasn't as bad as it looked.

"I can't believe they haven't called an ambulance yet," Beth murmured.

"Jay said it was going to be okay," Meg said. "Besides, how would they call an ambulance? There aren't any phones."

"They're rich. Bet you any amount of money they have a helicopter hidden somewhere in that forest." Beth shook her head and dropped her hand. There were only a few drops of blood smeared on it, only a few glittering shards of the chandelier left, and Meg didn't mention either of them because it wasn't important. Maybe it was important in the long run, but not enough when Kendra yelled from the other room before hissing out through her teeth loud enough Meg could hear it a room over.

She was lucky. She was so, so, so lucky that there were only a few drops of blood on her and none on Beth. It could have been so much worse.

"Hey," Beth said sternly, "I know that look. Buck up. We're in this, now."

"I thought you wanted out," Meg said, then bit her tongue. Stupid. She didn't want Beth to leave, especially not now.

"Well, yeah. But you don't," Beth said, like it was obvious, and then sobered and glanced up, same as Cal had done.

"Also," she said quietly, "Chandeliers don't just fall. Not like that."

"...You believe me."

Beth breathed out heavily. "You're getting a hell of a lot of proof. Come on." She helped her stand—it was stupid, since she wasn't actually hurt, but it sure felt like she needed it. Her legs wobbled with realization, with *I was so close* occupying her mind. "Let's go back up to your room. We'll talk more there."

Meg nodded, leaning on her gratefully, but something caught her attention: a dark smudge on the floor. Something that had been dropped and forgotten in the scuffle.

She paused, pulling away from Beth's hold just enough to get her to slow down; Beth's stop was immediate, on full alert. "What?"

"Nothing. Nothing, just... hold on." She glanced up out of reflex, to see if anyone had come around the corner to check on them, but no one seemed to have noticed they were missing yet. There was low murmuring from behind the wall, and another muffled cry of pain. Everyone was focused on Kendra, as they should have been, her and Beth all but forgotten.

Upon closer inspection, it looked like a wallet, and since it was black nobody had noticed it to pick it up. Definitely Kendra's, since it was in the thick of the shattered glass. She would have to give it to her.

She shakily picked it up; it was slim in her fingers, slim enough that it wouldn't be of much use as an actual wallet. Maybe it was Jay's, then?

She flipped it open to see, and nearly dropped it in shock.

Inside were only two things: an ID that said *Kendra James,* and a police officer's badge.

Chapter Twelve

Meg sat on her bed and stared at the ID in her hands. In the hours that she had tried to make sense of it, since the sun came up and that hunted feeling faded so that she could think straight, she still couldn't figure out which parts of Kendra and Jay's stories were real and which were lies. The ID looked real enough, but then she had never stared this closely at one before. Maybe it was a well-made fake? And the badge...

Her head hurt. This was much deeper than she could have imagined.

"Okay," Beth said, pacing in front of her, hands weaving through her hair and braiding absently. "First things first. Do we think that's real or... or some kind of weird joke? Could it be a prop?"

"Why the hell would she bring an extra fake driver's license with her?" Meg turned it over in her hands. "The real question is... why she hid this one, if it's her real one."

Beth gestured to the second half of the wallet: the police badge. It was shiny and looked brand new, and Meg couldn't for the life of her tell if *that* was real or not. But, again, she couldn't think of any circumstances where she would have a fake one.

"I don't like this," Meg murmured, but at the same time she set her shoulders, felt a new responsibility settle on them. Another question that needed answering. Another piece to the puzzle that she felt was coming together around her—although sometimes she didn't know if she was the assembler or just another piece.

At least this time, the answer would be easier to get. If Kendra was truly a police officer, she would tell the truth: because she had hidden this, and now they had it.

"I'm going to go talk to her," she said, standing and pocketing the wallet. "She should be awake now. And she's going to give me some answers, real ones, because I know something she's hiding."

Beth breathed out heavily and put her head in her hands. "We're blackmailing a police officer now," she muttered. "Great. Exactly what I was hoping to do this weekend."

"Well, when you put it like that it sounds bad," Meg said, sighing too. "Okay. I'm going to do this."

Beth stood up, too, though, and put a hand on her arm in warning.

"You can still back out," she said, her voice coming faster. There was still blood under her fingernails, black and crusted, and it twisted Meg's stomach in knots. People weren't meant to have that on their skin. "We should back out. We don't even know this girl. The police are here to investigate Cal. And you know me, I don't think there are things people can't control, but... but something's *wrong* with this house! Tell me you see that!"

She did. There was no arguing against it, not anymore, not when Kendra's face was cut open and every time she saw it, there was a part of her that whispered that she should be dead. That maybe Meg should be dead with her.

But it didn't matter if she had never met Eliza; she *felt* alive, still. She was here in this house, in every untouched room, in every beautiful thing that had been broken open and left to rot, in every pause and flicker of something deep in Cal's eyes.

She was dead. And someone was responsible. And that someone was going to pay, because Meg felt her eyes on her in this house and she would feel it for the rest of her life if she gave up now.

"We'll be safe," she said in a breathless whisper. "We'll be fine. We're so close."

Beth shook her head and let Meg lead her out of the room. It felt like walking out onto the battlefield.

It wasn't hard to find the makeshift infirmary—it was where everyone had gathered. Jay was the first one to catch Meg's attention, because even though he had been easy to gloss over in the group, something had dimmed since last night. He sat in a chair outside his wife's room with his head in his hands, a few extra bandages in his lap, scrubbing at hair that was still damp from the shower he had taken earlier. He looked up when Meg and Beth showed up, but when Beth gave him a courteous hello he just nodded and turned his attention back to the door.

Like he's keeping watch, Meg realized. In light of what she was carrying, it seemed less like a concerned husband thing to do and more like a partner. Otherwise, normal people would be in there.

"Good morning," Mr. Arud said. There were dark circles under his eyes that certainly weren't there when he was greeting them yesterday. "There's some food on the dining room table if you want breakfast. How are you feeling?"

Meg shrugged, in *how do you think,* and glanced at Cal instead of his father. "Is she up?"

"Up, but resting," Jay said quietly. There was something guarded in his eyes. Someone who suspected something and didn't plan on moving his back from the wall. "She's exhausted."

"I understand. I was just hoping to... see for myself that she's okay. Is that alright?"

After a moment more of hesitation, of him studying her expression to see if she would back down, Jay relented and nodded. "Only a few minutes."

Just like they had planned, like they had been doing it for years, Beth struck up a conversation with Cal and Mr. Arud to distract them, and Meg went in to see Kendra.

Kendra was resting on a small bed that looked to have been dragged from elsewhere with pillows propping her upright, and her eyes had been closed but they opened now—or at least the one Meg could see. The chandelier had struck the left side of her face, and the whole thing was taped over and covered in gauze, all the way down to her lips. It made her look even more severe, which she hadn't thought was possible.

"Meg," she said in greeting, not even pretending to be friendly.

"Hello," Meg said cautiously, and after a second of indecision she shut the door; when she turned back to Kendra, her body language had immediately changed. Her shoulders were straighter, her hands on top of the blanket and clenched like she was ready to throw it off and sprint (or fight), and her one eye was analytical and steady on her every move.

She was definitely the person the badge said she was.

"How are you feeling?" Meg asked, just to keep up appearances, and offered a smile. "Are you going to be able to use your eye again? I know Jay has medical experience, but... I would feel better hearing it from you."

Kendra relaxed marginally. Nothing actually moved, she just breathed out fully for once. "Yes, I will. I was lucky. I think a centimeter more and I'd have to wear an eye patch, which would be... more attention than I want."

"At work, right?" Meg asked, moving away from the door. Hopefully Beth would find a way to let her know if someone was eavesdropping or coming to intervene, maybe drop something. All she knew was that the wallet and badge felt very heavy in her pocket. "Where do you work?"

A pause.

"...At a grocery store."

Meg took the wallet out and showed it to her. She pursed her lips, fists tightening again, but didn't say anything.

"Try again," Meg said. "Don't worry, nobody's listening. Beth would let us know."

Kendra tilted her head. "Why don't you tell me who *you* are first?" she said instead. "Because right now, I know less about you than you know about me."

"I'm a person who found this after you dropped it." Meg shrugged, made to throw it back to her, and stopped herself. Just because she spoke with authority didn't mean she had it. If she handed it back, she lost her leverage. She lost her answers, which were in precious short supply. "That's all. So what is a police officer doing here?"

"Keep your voice down," Kendra said sharply, and leaned forward. "We're here investigating. Jay is my real husband. They wouldn't exactly let a detective in, even if we did win the auction fair and square."

"Which you didn't."

"Not exactly. We called in some favors from Jay's work." Her eye narrowed. "Like you did. How *did* you do that?"

Meg shook her head. She wasn't going to tell her anything until she knew why she was here. If she told the wrong person, she could blow her chances of finding any answers. "We're talking about *you*. Why are you here?"

Kendra paused again, trying to figure out if she could be intimidated out of it, and when Meg managed to keep her face steady she glanced down. Conceding defeat.

"We're investigating the death of his fiancée a year ago," she said.

Meg's heart jumped. "Really?"

"Yes. We had very little convincing proof a year ago, so it was ruled an accident, but some... evidence, came forward recently. We have reason to suspect he was involved."

Meg stared at her. "That's... why Beth and I are here. We found your evidence. The videos. That was us."

Kendra stared back at her a second, then hissed out through her teeth and put her head in her hands. "You're the girl."

"The girl who was brushed off, you mean," Meg retorted, stung. "Yeah. That was me. And when you didn't listen to me, I got my best friend and we went looking."

"Why?"

"Because… he's a murderer." Meg swallowed. Saying it out loud, it gave it more weight. Made it real. Before, it was her and Beth's crazy delusion. Out loud, it was dangerous. "We went to find something you could use."

"You're awfully devoted to getting justice for a woman who was dead long before you knew her," Kendra said. Her gaze was piercing, and it should have looked trusting but didn't. She had the demeanor of someone who was used to picking out lies and reasons, making the world into something that made sense. "Or did you know her?"

"No. I found the video at a garage sale last month. I didn't mean to get so involved, but…" Meg took a deep breath. "You saw it. It's not something you just… push to the side and forget about. Not if there's a chance it's real."

"I didn't think—" Kendra caught herself and took a deep breath, lowering her voice to a whisper. "We didn't think you'd lie your way into *staying at his house* if you actually thought he was a murderer!"

"You weren't listening to me!" Meg whispered back. "I was going to get more definitive proof and give it to you, to make you listen, and… things got carried away." Meg paused. It had all happened so fast, so sequential, so… easy, almost. She had just looked up and she was too far in to back out. "I didn't mean for it to get this far."

"Well, it's dangerous," Kendra said. The entire side of her face was taped over with gauze and she still thought Meg needed a warning. "So if you're smart, you'll use this to say you're not comfortable and get the hell out."

"I don't think he would—"

"There's no logical explanation for you to stay," Kendra interrupted, her voice firm. "Anyone in their right mind would get out after the house proved to be that unstable. I'm surprised Bill hasn't already packed his bags and run."

"He's a believer," Meg said. *And so am I.*

Kendra's one good eye narrowed. "This isn't a game," she said. "And you should get out before it becomes too real."

She knew what she was talking about. This was her job, not Meg's and Beth's, and she was telling them to get out, and yet...

And yet she couldn't leave. She couldn't. Not now.

"I'm staying," Meg said, tucking the wallet back into her pocket. Kendra just watched her, like she was a child throwing a temper tantrum, and the anger rooted itself in her head, in her gut. "Because I'm here, and my friend is here, because we thought we had to take things into our own hands since you wouldn't."

She turned and strode toward the door, ignoring Kendra calling her name.

There were answers here, waiting for her, and she intended to find them. She intended to see this through, because she had knowledge Kendra didn't, and tricks she couldn't use.

Chapter Thirteen

The good news was, counter to what Meg had expected, after one member of their party nearly died they were left alone. Cal and his father were focused on Kendra and Jay, and Meg didn't know what they were talking about but they were very focused on it. Maybe lawsuits, if the way Mr. Arud kept tightening his lips was any indication. Maybe the possibility of more danger, if the way Cal's eyes followed her with every step was.

Whatever the reason, nobody paid them any attention when they slipped out of the brightly-lit main room, past the empty dining room with more pre-made food laid out on it, past the makeshift infirmary where the rest of their party was gathered, past the kitchen that looked like it had never been used and was oddly bare of utensils and appliances, and toward the basement that made every hair on her arms stand on end.

There was a sandal down there, in this basement: the first sign she had had that Eliza had lived here at all. Nobody mentioned her. There were no remembrances or photos or gravestones on the property. It was like it all had been wiped clean... except that.

There might be more down there.

When they reached the basement, though, Beth stopped suddenly. "I'll stay here," she said. "I'll be your lookout."

Meg turned around and looked at her doubtfully, to which Beth just raised her hands in surrender. "Not chickening out," she said. "I swear. I want to be down there with you. But..." She paused and tilted her head slightly to indicate behind her; when Meg turned, Bill was there, shrinking back around a corner as soundlessly as he could. She didn't know what he was doing and she hadn't known he was there. "We have to be careful," she whispered.

Meg felt a prickle of fear run through her, but she couldn't let Beth see it. She squeezed her hand gratefully, trying not to dwell on it long enough that she lost her nerve, and slipped silently downstairs in the dark.

She took the stairs quietly, using her phone's flashlight to navigate, and stumbled onto the bottom floor; she could still hear Beth moving around at the top, behind the door. Hopefully she would hear whatever signal she gave in time to hide—even if the idea of hiding down here, in the dark, with the crow and God knew what else, set her teeth on edge. She couldn't see anything, but then she hadn't seen anything the first time either. The thought was far from comforting.

The tiny light illuminated more than Cal had shown them with the flashlight the night before. It wasn't an empty basement like it had seemed then—it was used for storage, like a normal house, and just around the corner she almost ran into a tower of empty cardboard boxes. It was the first sign of the modern world she had seen since she got here, an aberration from the careful atmosphere they cultivated. Almost as if they were hiding something.

Meg carefully sorted through them, trying not to make any noise or knock them over, but they were all empty. The address was for a PO box instead of their address, and some of them had packing lists still included but they were for miscellaneous items that didn't go together. A shelf to mount on the wall, a pair of scissors, a shovel, a handheld screwdriver set... a butcher block with kitchen knives.

She definitely hadn't seen that in the kitchen, when she was looking through it, and she hurriedly put the boxes back and spun around. No one had snuck up on her in the dark, but now she couldn't help but picture it that much clearer. Now, when the house settled and one of the boards creaked, she would picture Cal with a knife.

Focus. She couldn't afford to waste any more time looking for things about Cal—she needed to know about Eliza.

Even though she scanned, though, there was no sign of the white sandal. No presence, either, which maybe had something to do with the tiny glow she had to light her way. It wasn't much, but it was a shield, something she could hold in front of her and hide behind. It burned away a little of her fear.

She didn't have much time. Meg cast her light around, turning in circles. Who would have moved it? What would that mean for her, if someone else thought she knew the significance?

Danger. She felt it with each step, pressing in the small of her back, between her shoulders, on the edge of her skull, where her sliver of light couldn't protect her. Something in this dark was old and evil.

Stop that, she scolded herself, *you sound like Bill.*

Bill sounded a lot less crazy now.

Meg took a deep breath—the dust flooded her lungs—and then exhaled. "Get a hold of yourself," she whispered harshly. "*Look.*"

She turned in a circle again, slower, deliberately ignoring the feeling of eyes pressing into her back and looking at what was in front of her. And... there. In the corner, much harder to see now than she had originally thought, like it had gotten duller, but it was still there. Nobody was onto her.

She moved toward it and cast the light around with her phone for why it would be there of all places. It was so dark down here. So closed off. This was likely where they had thrown all of her stuff after she died. Like they could shut the memory of her out of the house, out of their lives, out of the ocean where she had been killed.

Maybe Cal had moved it. Maybe he would know if she disturbed it now, but...

She leaned down to look behind it and found what she had been hoping for: more of Eliza's things down here with it. There was a box, in the corner. The dust on top was so thick it crusted like gray snow.

Carefully, Meg knelt in front of it. It felt like a trap, to see who was curious enough to come down and disturb it. She could already see, when she ghosted her fingers over the side, that the cobwebs and dust stuck to her, stark against her skin. It was blood on her hands, evidence of her need to know what was in here.

She swiped her hand across the surface of the box. It had looked metal, but now she knew it was wood; it scraped rough against her palms. On top, in stark letters, it read DO NOT OPEN UNTIL. Underneath, someone had written a date in pen: *September 12, one year!*

A time capsule. Meg could remember doing one of those, too, when she and Beth were in middle school. The handwriting was elegant, a cross between regular and cursive lettering, and definitely done by a woman. Since Cal's mother wasn't in the picture, that meant this belonged to Eliza.

Meg's heart beat faster. She was here to uncover the reason behind Eliza's murder, but... but somehow, it hadn't hit her until now that she had had a life before she was a ghost to chase. This was something she had set aside because she was excited about the future—a future that had never come.

It was the start of evidence, what she had been looking for, but it was also going to hurt.

She carefully felt around the edges of the dusty box for a latch, and then eased off the lid.

Inside, there was a small collection of things: what had been important to her when she made it. A dried and pressed forget-me-not, the petals tiny and turning to dust against the bottom. A journal, the pages still crisp and unused, the title in block letters: *WEDDING PLANNER*. A family photo, her as a young adult and a group of others that had to be her parents and aunts and uncles, beaming with similar smiles. A photo of her and Cal, standing on the rocks where they had first met, his arms wrapped around her stomach and head on her shoulder while she laughed so hard she couldn't keep her eyes open for the camera. Meg had had the thought before that Cal didn't look like the murder had aged him the way she had expected, but here, at least, he looked much younger in his happiness, next to his radiant girlfriend, standing on the shore of his favorite place in the world.

Nothing was in the box that she had hoped for, though. It wasn't that it had been taken out, because the box hadn't been opened since it was made; it was that if Cal had had the thought back then, of killing her, Eliza had seen no sign of it. Nothing about it said she was afraid of him. She was a young girl in love—and planning, hoping, to marry him by the next year they were still together.

Meg carefully put everything back in and closed the lid as well as she could—not that it really mattered, all anyone had to see to find she had been snooping was the erased dust on the sides and the matching smudges on her fingers—and stood up with her flashlight. A waste of time. She couldn't believe, now, that she had been so afraid to come down here.

She cast around in the dark for anything else, something else that at least indicated Eliza had been alive, and her flashlight lit something oddly-shaped in the corner, nearly hidden in the thick dust and beneath the edges of the white sheets of a couch and chair. Something white, but she couldn't make out what.

Carefully, still listening for any signal from Beth that she needed to run, Meg moved toward it. Everything was so deathly tranquil down here that it set her on edge. No fresh air moving through from the crack under the closed door, no sign of the crow from earlier, no sign of life except the footprints in the floor where they had walked through last night and she had walked now.

She lifted the edge of the sheet, just barely and just with her fingertips, and looked at the unmistakable dull white, slightly yellowed edge of bone.

She recoiled, swallowed nausea and the urge to scream and run back upstairs—it couldn't be Eliza's bones, she was buried somewhere like a normal person—and lifted the sheet to get a full look.

Not bone: a full skeleton. A dog's skeleton. Small enough that it hadn't been fully grown when it died but not enough for being a puppy, all in one piece.

Curled up like it had been… been alive and just lied down and been picked clean as it lay there on the ground…

The dog from the video, she realized, and jolted up and to her feet, taking a few shaky steps backward. The video where Cal had been given a puppy and for a few minutes he had been the happiest person in the world. It was down here. Not buried like Eliza, but left down here to starve, or killed and the body left on the ground like it had never been alive in the first place.

Holding her breath to keep from screaming, holding her phone to make sure she didn't drop it, holding her panic at bay to keep her feet moving one in front of the other, Meg turned and fled.

Chapter Fourteen

Night came too quickly, so quickly Meg hadn't even gotten the chance to sleep deep enough to dream before Beth was in her room again, apologetically shaking her awake. She was silent, which seemed appropriate in the wake of what they had found. She was still shaken by it. All she could see were the bones, still all in one piece, still assembled like a puzzle someone had put together and left.

What kind of house is this?

"Hey," Beth said quietly, "You okay?"

Meg shook her head, but she got up anyways. She had slept in jeans; she felt watched, and everything else was a dress so she could evoke the memories of Eliza's sundresses, and she didn't want to press her luck any more than she had to. And besides, the cold kept wrapping around her when she managed to stop shivering, so it was easier to prepare to be cold than keep moving around. This house was so cold, and so silent that everything else echoed so that anything alive felt out of place. And now she understood why.

Because it was a tomb. It wasn't a house, because people didn't keep bones in houses.

"What are you thinking?" Beth asked.

She was thinking about how it was just as likely it had been dumped down there dead as it was to have curled up and died in its sleep as it was to have died in place because it was locked down there to die. She was thinking about how the only place that had proof Eliza had lived was the place where the sun didn't touch, like her entire presence had been wiped cleanly from the world. She was thinking about whether Eliza's bones were somewhere in the house, too.

Out loud, she said, "I wonder if the crow ate it."

"Stop it," Beth said, but her voice was shaky, and she grabbed Meg's hand and towed her out of the room; it brought her out of her mind, just a little, so she was grateful she wasn't gentle with her. "Stop it. We're not thinking about it anymore. We're not thinking about it because I can't have any more breakdowns, okay?"

Meg snorted, and when Beth grinned at her it was equal parts crazed and grateful.

By the time they got back to the main room—the blood and glass were gone, it was spotless, but it was too easy to focus on the spot that the chandelier had fallen and remember—everyone was assembled and waiting for them already. Meg wasn't surprised to find that Mr. Arud had joined them this time, or that Cal looked more collected than was normal, but she was surprised to see Bill, looking around him but not rattled. Not shaking. She knew he was a believer, but she had thought he would be smarter than to stick around where it was dangerous. The rest of them had reasons, but he was just a thrill-seeker, and that seemed a poor reason to risk his life.

"Good, you're all here. We should get going," Cal said, smiling as Meg and Beth joined the group. Meg wasn't surprised when Kendra moved toward her, subtly enough that Cal wouldn't notice. The gauze was half gone, the only part left on her temple under her bangs, but the rest of her face was blotchy red, and it made her look even angrier than usual.

"You really should get out," she whispered. "While you can. Before you get hurt, too."

Meg felt a prickle of fear. That sounded, from a police officer, awfully close to a threat—or an omen.

"And I told you I'm staying," she whispered back as Beth took up Cal and his father's attention with useless questions. "We're both staying. That's the end of it."

Kendra didn't say anything. Meg expected that was the closest she was going to get to a concession, so she pushed past her.

"So where are we going today?" Bill asked, and Meg couldn't tell if the excitement in his voice was false or not but it was at least quieter now. "Back to the basement?"

God, Meg hoped not. She squeezed Beth's hand to keep her nerve up. Now that she knew the bones were down there, it felt like she couldn't even muster the courage to go near them.

"We'll see." Cal looked up, like he expected another chandelier to fall, or another light to flicker out and leave them in darkness that breathed. "For now, we're going into the east wing."

The east wing. It was such an odd way of referring to his own house that Meg frowned. "And... we've been staying in the west wing, I take it?" How big was this house?

"Yes. It's not used very often, so I can't guarantee where we'll find something... or what we find. But it should be safe."

"Should be," Jay muttered, in something close to mutiny. He stuck close to Kendra, so close Meg suspected they were discreetly holding hands. She wondered if he had gone with her on jobs like this before, or if he would ever stop hearing that chandelier ripping down her face. She was up and moving, but the gauze was stark in the low light, and there would probably be a scar for the rest of her life.

This isn't a game, she thought, clearly, but if it made her stomach roil she couldn't let it stop her. Like she had told Kendra, it was entirely too late to back out.

"Nothing has ever happened like that before," Cal said, and started to lead them in the opposite direction of the night before. "I know you're worried, but... I know this house. It'll be fine."

That wasn't comforting, but it was apparently all they were going to get out of him. Beth shrugged at Meg and they followed him silently.

Whereas yesterday when they followed Cal there had been a tangible air of excitement in the silence, now Meg felt dread with every step she took, and it seemed she wasn't alone. Even Cal, who lived here, kept his head on a swivel, constantly looking. It disturbed Meg even more when she realized that there shouldn't have been anything to look for.

"Where are we going?" she asked, just to break the tense silence. "Which room?"

Cal's eyes darted over to her, and then forward again. There was no smile on his face this time, for one of the first times. He was tenser than she thought. "One of the guest bedrooms—"

Kendra stopped abruptly enough Meg ran into her shoulder before quickly moving away; just like that, the procession stopped, both Cal and his father turning around to give her their full attention. "What is it?" Cal asked as Kendra put a hand to the gauze on her face. "Are you okay?"

"Fine. Fine, it's nothing." Kendra straightened, her hand still over her eye and the bandage. It was hard to tell in the low light, but the bandage looked like it was turning dark again. Reopened. That was a bad sign. "I just moved wrong. I'm fine."

"Kens," Jay said, voice soft but firm, "What do you need?"

It was a simple phrasing, an easy question, but Kendra still hesitated. The whole group waited, but Kendra's face was drawn tight with pain and embarrassment, and Meg wasn't surprised when she exhaled heavily and leaned back on her husband.

"I don't think I'm up to this anymore," Kendra admitted under her breath, holding onto Jay. "I just... My head hurts. I don't think I should be moving this much. I'm sorry."

"It's alright. Take your time," Jay said, holding her by the shoulder, and then glanced up at Cal. "Could you come with us? I'm not sure I know the way back, and I have something I want to speak to you about."

Cal hesitated, glancing in the direction of the rest of the group, but nodded and broke apart from them. "Dad? Do you mind leading until I get back?"

"No, you go ahead."

Mr. Arud looked distinctly nervous, though, when Cal went with Kendra and Jay back in the direction of the infirmary. Realistically, with what Meg knew, they were trying to get evidence of a murder. They had just successfully separated their possible murderer from the rest of his group so they could question him alone. *Brilliant.*

But inconvenient. She glanced at Beth, who shrugged in a 'what are you going to do' motion and followed after Mr. Arud. Meg considered trying to follow after them, but Kendra had one of her secrets as leverage, too, so she decided she wouldn't risk it. Not this time.

"Alright," Mr. Arud said, a little too loud in the silence. It was Cal who knew the house, then. He seemed almost as nervous in the dark as the rest of them did. "He'll catch up to us again soon, I'm sure. I think the guest bedroom is a good place to start, too."

"Any particular reason?" Bill asked. "I didn't find anything about a bedroom in my research."

"It's difficult to say for sure," Mr. Arud admitted. "There are stories that have been told for over a hundred years. We don't know which ones are real and which are just that: stories."

"Tell us a story, then," Bill demanded more than suggested. Meg thought his enthusiasm needed to be toned down, considering the cemetery they were walking through. Even if he didn't know the actual truth, he had to at least feel it in the air. She was sure everyone could.

Mr. Arud hesitated; his leg with the limp dragged against the floor and scraped uncomfortably loud with the abruptness of it. "There are a lot of them."

Meg knew that. She had found them while she was looking for information on Cal, and she didn't want to hear them now, in the dark, isolated, almost alone. She knew all the stories already, the ones that made the house feel like it actually could be haunted. Why wouldn't it be, when you knew these stories? A haunted house needed a history, an air, and the belief that things were happening that couldn't be real. When she read them at home with Beth in her well-lit living room with the separation of a computer screen, they were almost funny.

Now that she was here, walking through this house's bones, breathing its ancient air, they were something else.

"There are stories dating back over a hundred years," Mr. Arud started, his tone taking the cadence of someone sitting at a campfire, a hushed and reverent whisper, "And I know that they're true because some of them are about my own family."

He said it so *casually*. "Stories about your own relatives?" Meg asked. She knew every family had their oddities and whispered secrets that were passed around at reunions and funerals, but they weren't the type to tell to strangers. Affairs and secret jobs and long-lost children, not murders.

"Some of them, yes. Everyone who has lived here has, at some point... seen something they can't explain." He stopped short, the rest of them stopping behind him. "And some of it that is... family lore. Like this spot. This is where Richard Arud—my great-great-uncle—died, right here in this hallway. Something had attacked him, but police were never able to figure out what."

"Why do you say 'what' and not 'who'?" Bill asked.

"Because the wounds were... odd. He was covered in scratches, especially his face, but nothing that should have killed him. And his cause of death was determined to be a heart attack. It doesn't make sense."

"I love finding things in your house that don't make any sense," she says brightly, holding up a piece of wood that looks like a stake. "Like this. Cal, why is there a stake holding the back door shut?"

"What, your family doesn't do that?"

"No, we use locks. Like modern people." She waves it again, insistently. "What's the story here?"

"That's because of one of the cats that got out." His voice drops as he takes it from her. "One of my great-aunt's cats was a mouser, here, so she let it in and out of the house. All day and night, apparently, you would just hear the door opening and closing."

"Ah. That sounds like a cat."

"Yes. Except that was thirty years ago, so the cat—and my great-aunt—are long gone. But at night, if you don't put something in front of it, the door will open sometimes. Even if it's locked." He tilts it sideways. There's a curve to the wood, as if it's been strained over the slow course of years. "She tries anyways. Sometimes she even succeeds."

"It's not just family that had experiences here, either. One of the other famous stories is of a maid that worked here in the fifties. She was running after a dog that got loose and went into the forest right before a big storm—she was missing all night. When they found her, right outside the house in the rose garden, she had blood on her hands. She kept going on and on about wings, said she had seen someone flying. When another maid ran in to get help, she vanished."

He paused for a breath, for the effect.

"And?" Bill prompted after a moment.

Mr. Arud gave a small shake of his head. "No one knows. All I know is... when you go in that rose garden, you feel watched."

"Who planted these roses?" she asks, putting one to her nose and inhaling. "They look like they've been here for years. Your mom, or before her?"

"Before her. Long before." He reaches out and grasps another one, the camera zooming in on the petals between his fingers, the dew that lingers on them, and brushes over the center with his thumb. "I believe they were planted by one of the gardeners who worked for my grandfather. He brought they with him when he came to work here. They were originally from his wife."

"That's so beautiful." She turns around. "And the gazebo? Was that him, too?"

"No. That was... in honor of him, actually. He died out here, in this garden. There was a windy night and he went out to check on the roses in the middle of the night and a tree fell on him. By the time they found him in the morning, he had passed away."

"Oh." She shakes her head, as if rejecting the imaginings of what might have happened. "That was nice, of your family."

"They all loved him. That was when the first fence was built, to keep people out of the forest if there was a storm, and then they built the gazebo and put some supplies inside so if there was an unexpected squall, there was somewhere safe to stay." The camera focuses on it, the paint peeling but the structure solid. "It was... basically their way of making sure it never happened again."

"This window here..." Mr. Arud cleared his throat, looked down. "Sorry, it's..."

They waited for him to compose himself, and then he turned around and pulled down the edge of his shirt. Meg could barely make out the edge of a scarred, slightly-raised mark on his neck, repaired by stitches, that went from the base of where it met his shoulders to out of sight on his chest. "There was a lightning strike during a really bad storm years ago that struck so close it blew the glass in. Most of the pieces went into my leg, but one of them impaled up here. If Cal hadn't been there... well. I might not be here."

"How old was he?" Meg asked.

Mr. Arud hesitated. "Eight."

Too young.

They sit in the grass, the camera set between them. It points at their hands, propping themselves up, and the slab of gray stone with flowers atop it is barely visible from the angle.

"You were young when she passed, right?" she asks softly.

"I was a kid, yeah." He shrugs slightly. "So it's... mostly stopped hurting."

"My mom died five years ago. It never stops hurting." She reaches out and takes his hand. "Thank you for showing me, Cal."

He squeezes her hand. "She died here, you know. In an accident. Slipped and fell down one of the staircases. Dad told me that... it would have been instant, and that's at least merciful."

"Maybe." She leans into him. "But that doesn't make it okay."

Unforgivable. All of it.

Meg bumped into Beth when she jerked to a sudden stop and squeezed her hand so hard her bones ached. "What is it?" Meg whispered. Nothing. "Beth?"

"I... don't know." Beth's face was twitching like she was battling down emotions one after the other. Mostly hysteria. She was looking over her shoulder behind them and it didn't make her feel any better that there was nothing there. "Did you hear that?"

"Stop it," Meg said, trying for light and teasing. Bill and Mr. Arud's complete silence in front of her made it sound forced. "Stop it. I didn't hear anything."

"I'm serious. I heard something moving over there!"

"Probably just the wind," Mr. Arud said, his calm businessman voice grating against Meg's nerves. "It's an old house, you know. Things creak."

"And break," Beth fired back, but she gave it only one more glance and then marched away. "Have you ever updated it? Is that in your history?"

"Of course. Most of the structure is original, but we had to update the utilities..."

Meg moved to follow her, but her feet rooted to the floor.

Something creaked behind her.

She froze in place and resisted the urge to turn back. *There's nothing there. Nothing at all. You're hearing things.*

But *why* was she hearing things?

Because you won't look. Because you're afraid you're wrong.

That felt cowardly, so Meg set her jaw and turned around, fast.

And caught the tail end of something moving out of the corner of her vision.

Something light, something wispy, something *alive.*

She backed up a step, quickly, stifling a scream behind her teeth. It was gone, but the imprint was still there, lingering in the dark, clear in front of her eyes, and she was so damn cold.

You're hallucinating, she would take that at this point, *you're going crazy, there's nothing actually there, you're just seeing things,* **get a hold of yourself—**

The floor collapsed beneath her feet, and she fell straight down into the dark.

Chapter Fifteen

Meg couldn't breathe.

It was like someone had stuffed her inside of a bag, inside of a box with no light and no air holes; everything was closed up at once. Choking. Her throat was tight. She was trying to scream but she couldn't make a sound.

Something rung in her ears. Maybe her screaming. Maybe someone else's. Mostly blood rushing, her own heart pounding, her own thrashing and beating like drums—

Can't breathe. Can't breathe. Can't breathe.

Her hands were moving, frantically, but they were separate from her body, they weren't finding anything. Couldn't get to her neck, she didn't know what was wrong with her neck, but it felt like hands around her windpipe, cruel, gripping tighter, tighter...

I'm going to die.

The thought sent a black tidal wave of panic through her, like something exploding in her lungs and up through her throat, and she thrashed harder. No. No. Not like this, not here, not now—

Air, she commanded herself. *Air.* **Breathe.**

Her mouth was opening and closing, she was aware of that because there was dust on her tongue, but something wasn't working. Something crucial wasn't working but she didn't know what. Everything was hazy. Fuzzy. Not functioning.

Meg gasped—maybe. She thought she was. She should have been. That was what... what happened in the movies...

There was darkness on the edge of her vision, a darkness deeper than the black around her, more menacing, more permanent. Her eyes were closed—no, they were open, there was dirt in them, but she couldn't see anything.

No, no, no...

She fell, her body light and weightless and unanchored from her mind, and that permanent darkness swept up and closed cruelly over her.

Meg breathed in.

The air burned. It felt sharp going down her throat, like swallowing knives, and she coughed and hacked and struggled to help it reach her lungs.

What... What...

She cracked her eyes open—why had they been closed in the first place?—and looked up at the gray-black of the dark ceiling. She was in Cal's house, that was right... but that didn't explain why everything hurt, or why her limbs were full of cement.

Wait. Someone was here. Someone else was breathing hard, and she was leaning against them.

She turned her head—it sent a twinge up her neck—to look at the person holding her.

It was Cal. He held her mostly upright, hands gently supporting her back and neck, which throbbed insistently with each breath, like an invisible giant had her in a chokehold. When she put her hand to her throat it was damp, but she couldn't tell if it was with sweat or blood.

It *burned,* inside and out.

"You're okay," he said, and his voice was hoarse. Like it was the first time she was hearing it, but not the first time he had said it out loud. "You're okay. Just take your time."

Meg shut her eyes and searched her memory. Where had Cal come from? Why did everything hurt?

All she remembered... was falling.

She wasn't looking at the ceiling at all. That was the ceiling from the floor above, through a hole in the floor, and her arms and legs and the skin on her stomach were scraped raw from the rough edges of the wood.

"The floor collapsed," she managed. "But..."

Her throat. She still couldn't get her head to stop spinning.

"Old wiring," Cal said, a little breathlessly. "In the ceiling. It got tangled around your throat. But you're safe now."

So he said. So Meg tried to tell herself over and over, but her body wouldn't shut off the adrenaline. She couldn't stop *shaking*.

"Just breathe," Cal said softly. "Breathe. It's over. You're safe."

It felt like it was still around her throat. She felt it, every time she breathed.

"You're okay. I promise."

And then she heard the shouting coming from behind them, people who had finally found a way down (she had fallen, that was right—) and something else clicked: Cal had gotten to her the fastest. He must have sprinted. He must have known the fastest way to get here and used it.

She might be dead if he hadn't.

"Meg?!" Beth yelled.

Meg opened her mouth to answer, but all that came out was more coughing, deep and hard enough to shake her whole body until her vision spun. The air that was coming up was stale, and clogged with thick, old dust.

"Over here," Cal called back for her.

"Meg!" Beth ran through the door, tears already starting in her eyes, a look of pure panic, and took Cal's place holding her up in a hug. "Oh my god, I'm sorry, I—I didn't even realize you weren't right behind me, are you okay?"

She would've been more okay if the hug didn't feel like clamping a vice on her lungs, but she didn't have it in her to say it. Beth held her by the shoulders tightly, and Meg couldn't tell if it was her who was shaking or both of them. Feeling was still coming back into her limbs.

"I'm..." *Fine.* No, she wasn't. She took a deep breath that hiccuped. "I'm..."

Beth hugged her again, and Meg accepted it gratefully. "Is there any place in this house that isn't a *death trap?*" she demanded of Cal. "What the hell is *wrong* with this place?"

"I... This has never happened before—"

"You said that with the chandelier." Now that she was listening, Beth's voice wasn't furious. It was shaky, on the verge of hysterics, and Meg almost shook too because she had never been somewhere that *felt* so malicious. She had never been so afraid of where she set her feet or waited for everything to grow arms and grab her. "And now it's happened with the floor. What's next?!"

"Wasn't his fault," Meg rasped. Whatever else he had done, he had saved her from choking to death. "Just... an accident."

Beth breathed out harshly. "Yeah, I know. Just..." She paused, glancing up at the ceiling like she expected something else to come out of it. But she didn't finish the thought. Just shook her head. "Come on. Let's get you looked at. Your throat looks like hell."

Hurts like it, too. She just nodded. She still felt shaky, barely breathing.

"The infirmary is getting a lot of use this weekend," Cal said, sounding oddly resigned.

For a moment, Meg had actually forgotten he was there. His presence didn't feel threatening right now, compared to everything else—not after what had just happened.

You saved my life, she wanted to say, it was on the tip of her tongue, but it got lost somewhere. How he was staring at her, with total fixation, with dimming panic since he saw her breathing. She could still feel his hands gripping her shoulders. Still hear the desperation in his voice.

She didn't know how she felt about it, but she couldn't push it away.

"Come on," Beth said quietly, arm around her shoulders. Meg could still feel the tremors. "You'll feel better after you sleep."

Chapter Sixteen

Meg didn't sleep. Every time she tried, the memory of that darkness and the smell of the dust closed around her, and her eyes jerked open and she was gasping for air and clutching at her sheets. Every time, even when she tried to brace herself, she shuddered and held a hand over her mouth so she didn't scream and wake everyone else up. One time she ended up in the corner of the room, curled up over her stomach, absolutely sure she was going to pass out, but after ninety-two seconds she normalized. She was breathing. She was alive.

Her throat hurt. Every move, she was aware of it. It hurt so much, burned so clearly in the exact marks that the wires had left, that she was sure she'd be aware of it for the rest of her life.

Finally, she crawled out of bed and shuffled out of her room. When she swung her door open, fast, before she could change her mind, it ran into something solid.

"Ow!" Beth sprang to her feet, startled, and blinked at her. "You're up."

Meg stared at her, pieces clicking into place. "You were... sleeping out here?"

Beth shrugged and crossed her arms. "It made me feel better."

Meg smiled, touched by her care, and maybe she was still emotional from the near-death experience but she swept Beth up in a hug that was as big as she could manage. Beth returned it, holding onto her with both hands like she was going to disappear if she let go.

"Thank you," Meg whispered. Her throat was still raw, but that wasn't why she teared up.

Beth nodded into her shoulder. "I can't protect you from much, but I can protect you from him," she whispered back.

Cal. Meg understood why she was protective, he was the reason they were here in the first place and it was his house that kept nearly killing her, but she couldn't stop seeing his face leaning over her when she gasped back into life. He had been so panicked and pale, had made the choice to run and save her when no one else could have.

And he had said her name like a drowning man finding the shore. With much more emotion than she was used to thinking of murderers as having.

"Are you okay?" Beth asked, pulling back and pushing Meg's hair behind her ear; it bared her neck to the cold air so she flinched, and she withdrew her hand immediately. "Do you need anything? Painkiller? Water? A double-barrel shotgun and a gallon of liquor?"

Meg laughed—regretted it, but laughed. It was worth it for the tentative smile Beth gave her. Meg was sorry she couldn't offer more.

"Need to walk," she said.

Need answers.

The air outside was heavy, but it was clean, and that was all Meg was looking for. Something that chased away the lingering, clinging memory of falling through the floor. Her room was relatively clean, since it was used, but it was still the house. It still... smelled like it. That was what kept waking her up: the smell that hung in the air above her bed. Dust and damp wood and old paint. It was what had flooded into her mouth when she gasped for air, and if she breathed in too deeply she remembered what it had been like to feel it stop under her skin and not reach her lungs.

Breathing in the salt, she didn't remember it as clearly, so she could just breathe.

This time, Meg felt Cal's presence before she felt his hand on her waist; she was becoming attuned to him. Not in a good way, though, that she could call familiarity. In the way an abused child learned to feel for a raised temper.

And yet, he had saved her life.

"You didn't try to attack me that time," he said, sounding amused. "I must be losing my touch."

"Is that what I was trying to do?" She didn't bother to look at him, or to disguise the rasp in her throat. Every word was like swallowing a knife blade-first. "I thought I freaked out."

"A little of both, I think. I would've deserved either one."

He stood next to her on the cliff, hands in his pockets as if the height didn't bother him at all, like the edge wouldn't dare give in on him. They were close enough their shoulders nearly brushed until Meg moved away so she could rub her arms without touching him. She was back to the white dress; it was all she had left. After nearly dying yesterday, she didn't want to take any chances with Cal, too.

Although maybe calling up the ghost of a murdered girl wasn't the smartest idea, either. Maybe that was where she went wrong in the first place.

"How's your throat?" Cal asked quietly.

Meg shrugged. "Better than last night." She touched the edge of her neck, just out of habit; the ridges were pronounced, and sharp, folded into her skin and raw to the touch. Basically burns on the outside of her neck, like a choker. She didn't know if they would scar. She hadn't really thought that far yet. She was going one day at a time.

"I'm sorry. I shouldn't have asked." Cal looked pointedly out at the water, hands still folded in his pockets but his shoulders hunched forward against the cold. "...I'm sorry."

"Not your fault." Meg kept her own hands out, but this time she didn't feel the need to curl her fingers and brace herself. This was as close to a normal conversation as she had ever had with him. And the other thing. "You saved my life. I should be thanking you."

He was silent for a long time, his eyes flickering out over the ocean like he was picking out things Meg couldn't see. The look on his face was... oddly involved. Almost guilty.

"Still," he said at last. "It was my house. I'm sorry."

"You can't control everything in it." But her mind flashed back to Beth, crouched next to her and looking up at the chandelier hook that had given out right over her and Kendra's heads, gaze troubled. *Chandeliers don't just fall. Not like that.*

And floors didn't just give in. Not like that. She shuddered but not from the cold.

Next to her, Cal took off his coat and handed it to her wordlessly. She couldn't think of a tactful way to turn him down so she took it and put it on gratefully.

"I can't control everything in it. But that doesn't stop me from apologizing. It's been... unusually volatile, this trip." He laughed once, but there was no humor in it. "Not sure those waivers are going to stand this time."

He was skirting around something. Meg felt it, in the silence: there was something he wanted to say but he couldn't find the words or the will to get around the block. Something stopped him.

Only one way to find out.

"Want to walk?" she asked him, tilting her head towards the beach, where the waves were pulling in and out a few slow inches at a time.

When he smiled back and gestured for her to lead the way, Meg felt for the fear, listened for its ring in her ears, braced for the drop in her stomach.

She felt nothing.

The tide was coming in. Meg wasn't sure exactly when, in the three days she had seen this ocean, she had learned to read it enough to know that, but she knew now. Something about the way the water sounded against the rocks, maybe. She could see a storm brewing on the edge of the horizon, but that wasn't the reason she felt like the water pulling in had a vengeance to it. It hit the rocks like it was trying to ground them into sand, with much more force than going in. She heard the distance. She felt it.

The ocean's moods were volatile, but she had expected it. She had known the storm was coming in. She could handle this, the same way she apparently could handle nearly being choked to death by a vengeful house that didn't want memories of Eliza to live.

Mentally, she braced herself for the storm, but it dropped a sense of calm over her like she had never experienced. A kind of tranquility like everything was happening outside of her and beating harmlessly against her skin.

"You move like you've walked on beaches your whole life," Cal murmured. Maybe it was meant to be a compliment, but Meg was pretty sure he was lying. She was far from graceful, even if she didn't feel as immediately that the rocks were going to impale her. She had to work to keep her legs from trembling underneath her every time they listed.

There was a driftwood tree in their path, roots curled in all directions like bleached lightning; Cal took her hand to help her over. His own skin felt as soft as hers, which she had never noticed before. Most men had calluses, or sun damage, but Cal's was as smooth as if he had just lived in the house for his whole life.

He knows the house better than anyone else alive.

She still knew so little about him, in spite of everything he had told her.

"So," she said, discreetly pulling her hand back; he let it happen, putting his hands in his pockets, which she thought was brave given the rocks they were walking on. "Have you lived here your whole life? Your dad said you knew the house the best."

"At first just summers, back when my mom was still alive." His eyes flickered with memory, just for a split second, but cleared almost immediately. So it had happened long enough ago that the sorrow of a death was just a momentary echo in his mind, a hole so old that he had to stumble upon it to remember it was there. "We went on trips a lot, but we came here every summer, and I knew every inch of the property like the back of my hand. The house was mostly empty, and mostly the same as when it was first built, so I loved it. When I got older, and I had choices, I just... liked it here better than our other home."

"There a reason?"

He shrugged. "It had more personality, for one thing." The corner of his mouth twitched, like it was a phrase his family passed around a lot. It had so much presence Meg believed it. "New houses are just too clean. No secrets, no stories, no quirks for a kid to discover. Plus, I love the water. I don't go in it very much, it's freezing cold and the riptide is killer, but I love just standing out here and listening to it when it picks up." He paused a second, glanced at Meg, and then looked back out. "Plus, the view is nicer."

Her skin heated up, but she didn't reply. Right now she didn't have the energy to keep up the act of being in love with him like Eliza was.

Eliza. It was hard thinking of even her name right now, in light of everything that had happened. How much had she seen in the short year she was here? How much of the house had creaked when she stepped, how much had collapsed under her feet, how much had welcomed her as much as it welcomed Cal? How much of Cal had she loved and how much had seemed blank and unknown, like he was slipping into someone else's persona?

How had it felt for her to die, Meg wondered with a shudder that crawled up her spine like something alive. She just hoped that it was quick, that she hadn't even realized she was falling before she hit the ground.

She hoped she didn't realize who had pushed her at all.

"What are your best memories of this beach?" she asked, whispering because it didn't scrape as harsh against her throat. She was tired of being afraid and dancing around the right questions. She wanted answers, and this was as fragile and real as she had seen Cal yet. If she was going to get answers, it was going to be now. "Tell me something you love."

Cal's eyes shadowed, pulling away from the memories she was digging up, and Meg took a step toward him. "Cal," she said quietly, seeing his lashes flicker like he was resisting the urge to close his eyes against her, "Please. Tell me something about yourself."

He sucked in a deep breath and let it out suddenly, rubbing the back of his head, and Meg was struck, for the first time, by how young he looked. How boyish the motion was, when he looked out to sea to avoid looking at her. He was her age. The act of murder aged someone, so she had thought of him as older than her. Someone whose experiences made him an inherent stranger, someone she could never hope to connect with or understand.

Right now, he looked strikingly similar to someone she would have gone to school with, or work with, or fallen in love with.

"I was engaged once," he said quietly, still looking out over the water, his hands shoved into his pockets and shoulders hunched. "To a girl I met here, on this beach. Eliza. She lived on the coast a few miles away, and one day, on a whim, she walked all the way here. It was... instant, the connection between us. I felt like I had known her my whole life." A pause, in which he didn't look at her, didn't speak, didn't move a muscle, then— "We were... going to have an August wedding. I couldn't wait to spend the rest of my life with her."

Meg's face was frozen, with the proximity to him, with the possibility of him turning to look at her in an instant; her insides, though, turned and turned and turned. Disgust, at how he could look out at the sea like someone struggling with inconsolable loss when she had watched him push her off the cliff. Pity, at how lost he seemed, at how she had chalked up to ease the fact that he didn't look at the rocks at his feet and she was just now understanding that they would be red for him, too.

Confusion, at how easily she felt pity for a murderer, and how genuine the tearing apart on his face felt.

"What happened?"

For a long time, he didn't answer. Just looked out at the ocean like it held memories he was trying to bring to the surface.

"She died," he said finally, voice flat. "Died right here on this beach, and... and I found her body. The ocean was almost taking her out to sea by the time we got down there, so..." He paused. "There was seaweed in her hair. Seaweed in her hair, like when we used to go swimming, so... so I almost just thought she was asleep and floating on her back. Like we used to do."

"She... fell?"

"Slipped." His gaze moved up, to the cliff that loomed tall over them. "From up there. She just said she wanted to watch the sunset, and then..."

Liar, Meg's mind reminded her, because she wanted to hate him, she did, but he looked trapped by the memories.

"I'm sorry," she said, because it was all she could think of. And she really was, for Eliza.

Cal didn't look at her. Continued to look up at the cliff, his hair moving in the slight breeze, his eyes studying it even though he had to have seen it a million times. He must see this place in his sleep, no matter how much he wanted not to. He must miss her—Or, no. Or...

She was tired of all of this. There was something wrong here and... and she wanted to go home and breathe without her lungs seizing up because the air was too full of things she couldn't put names to. She wanted to turn her back without feeling eyes when she was alone. She wanted her brain to stop rattling, stop panicking, stop inventing things to fear, stop wondering what was going to happen to her or Beth next.

She could leave and come back when—if—it stopped hurting with every breath and heartbeat. She could leave and come back after watching the videos so that her resolve would be strong again.

"What are you thinking?" Cal asked quietly.

Meg looked back at him, trying to make her decision. He had the same look on his face as when she had resurfaced from choking: like she was beautiful, and so, so important, and he was afraid to look away from her.

How could he be a murderer?

Her head hurt.

"I think I need to go home," she admitted, smiling so wide it hurt her throat to take the edge off the words. "I'll come back, but I've had enough excitement for one weekend."

Cal's face softened, and he glanced back over the water. Then up to the sky, which was closing up on them like a second sheet of rolling waves. "Then you may want to hurry," he said. "Storm's coming in."

Hurrying was the right thing, but the front was already above them, and the wind already picking up, so Meg stood still and faced forward with him. They stood in silence and watched it darken the ground at their feet, ripple over the water crashing closer and closer toward them and whip the waves higher, and the first raindrops were like bullets against her skin: strikes, abrasive and cold, picking up in intensity as they continued to fall.

And that was just the beginning of it. The clouds over the water, coming towards them like a freight train, were rumbling with carrying thunder and black enough to blot out the sun.

Chapter Seventeen

When the storm hit, it hit like a bomb going off.

Meg and Cal barely got back to the house before the sky turned black like someone had flipped a light switch on the sun, and she had only made it up to her room to try to pack before the rain started. Not just started, but gone from nothing at all to hitting the windowpanes hard enough she wondered if it could break them. She backed away, a little in awe. Where had that *come from?*

Beth walked in without knocking. Her face was tight with stress, and she moved to Meg's side. "I thought we had another hour."

"So did I." Meg couldn't stop staring. It was both awe-inspiring and terrifying, how fast it had struck. Hadn't she just seen the sun?

Beth pursed her lips together and steered her away from the window. "Dammit," she muttered. "Terrible timing."

Meg laughed weakly. "Someone's conspiring against us, I think."

"Stop that. Stop that, bad luck is about all I can handle right now."

She spun around, putting Meg behind her as the door opened; it was Cal, who smiled apologetically. "I didn't mean to startle you. I just wanted to make sure you were both okay."

"We're fine," Beth said, harsher than she needed to. "It's just a storm. Never hurt anybody."

"I didn't say it would," Cal replied, voice level, an actor's voice if Meg had ever heard one, and he offered Meg a small smile that Beth tensed at like she wanted to deflect it away. "But this is a fiercer one than usual. I know you were hoping to leave, but... I really don't suggest it. The roads out of here aren't the best."

Meg breathed out, dread pooling in her stomach. "My car's not even four-wheel drive," she whispered to Beth. "And this is a dirt road. I don't think we'd get very far."

"If the road isn't blocked off already." Mr. Arud joined them slowly, almost against his will, with his hands in his pocket and his head pivoting from window to window as they rattled. He looked like he hadn't slept in days.

"The forest," he said in explanation and apology both, "It's old, and it was a hot summer so a lot of the trees are weak. If one isn't down within half an hour, I'd be shocked. If they're not already falling."

In which case driving out in it, she was more likely to get them both killed than staying in this house—even if it did sound more appealing. Meg glanced at Beth, who glowered at both Cal and his father. "You say that like it's a good reason to stay someplace we almost died. Twice!"

"It'll be fine—"

"*Twice!*"

"Beth, I'm alive." It was amazing how not-comforting that was. "It's fine. It'll be fine."

"It is *not* fine." She raised her voice. "Jay, I know you're listening! Tell me you're not itching to get out of here, too!"

There was a moment of silence, and then, sure enough, Jay appeared from around the corner, and she heard the footsteps and creaking floorboards that meant Kendra and Bill were close behind them. They must have been in their rooms, just through a thin wall. She had felt very alone just a few minutes ago and it didn't settle her nerves to know she had been wrong.

The windowpane behind her shook with the wind and rain trying to tear through and get them; the others didn't turn toward it, didn't seem to pay any attention to it, but it was all she was aware of for a second. She wasn't sure what she wanted to be at the mercy of less, the house or the storm or the people inside of it.

Jay fixed Beth with a look that Meg recognized from her dad. The 'calm down and consider what you're saying' look. "I understand you're concerned," he said, and Meg was almost convinced that he was calm except the way he clenched his fists at his sides. "I'm concerned, too. But we can't control what the weather does. All we can control..." And here he looked over at Cal, who was so still he might not have been breathing at all. "Is what happens in this house. So, to avoid any more accidents, I suggest we choose one place to hunker down and wait out the storm."

Bill opened his mouth like he was going to say something, then closed it and shook his head. Even he recognized that this wasn't the time to suggest they go exploring. Meg was glad for that.

"The house isn't dangerous," Mr. Arud said, and glanced at Cal. "These are accidents, nothing more."

"Still," Jay said. "I suggest we don't encourage any more accidents."

He stared Mr. Arud down, daring argument, but he got none. Cal held out his hand in an invitation for him to lead the way to 'somewhere safe,' and the ease with which he dismissed their worries about his house would have been enough to start something if Kendra hadn't grabbed her husband's hand. Her face was pale, and Meg didn't think it was an act, so they just left quietly.

Jay stuck close to Kendra's side, and Beth hung next to Meg, and nobody said anything when the rain picked up and lightning struck so close its charge seemed to race through her veins.

There was no leaving tonight.

In retrospect, Meg would have preferred to take her chances on the house killing her over sitting in a silent circle around the dining room table.

That was the only place Jay had deemed safe enough (Kendra seemed a bit fed up with his over-protectiveness, but just enough that Meg could tell she didn't really mind) since they had been sitting in it for meals the whole time and nothing had happened, and nobody had argued, even Bill. Maybe he worried he would be next. Meg didn't blame him.

They sat without talking, too tense to try to act normal, and listened to the storm rage outside. This one was a good one, the kind everyone had been bracing for all summer without knowing they were: the one that when it was over, you looked for a body count. Meg kept hearing things breaking, snapping, coming off in great bursts of noise outside. Trees. Branches. Cracks of lightning. Parts of siding off the house. Everything was trying to rip itself apart above her head, and she couldn't help but feel it a little personally. The house was already dangerous; now it was gaining extra ammunition.

And then the lights all went out at once.

Beth gasped and grabbed for Meg's hand; Meg didn't even feel surprise, anymore. Only resignation, so deep it felt like dread.

Cal jumped to his feet. In the low light, it was hard to see his face, but the edges of it were harsh, like the shadows had made themselves at home inside of him, and he didn't look panicked. "The power's out."

Beth breathed out harshly. "Just what we needed."

"It's expected," Bill said in an attempt at comfort. "It's an old house and we're in the middle of nowhere—although now that I think about it, I didn't see any power lines. Where does your power come from?"

"We have lines connecting from the roof to the shed. There's a generator there." Mr. Arud backed up a step from the rest of them. "It fails in heavy winds, if they're strong enough."

"Of course it does," Beth said, standing up too. "But that doesn't mean I want to sit here and freeze in the dark all night. What can we do to fix it?"

Cal chewed on the inside of his cheek. "The generator could just need restarting, or the power could need to be reset from inside the house."

"So we should check both places." Jay nodded. "Mr. Arud can go look outside, and Cal can look inside."

"We shouldn't go anywhere alone," Kendra said quietly. "If something happens, with the storm or the house, we may not be able to find each other in the dark."

Bill breathed out. "Alright. I'll go with Mr. Arud outside. I have a generator on my ranch. If it's broken, I may be able to help."

Kendra sent a deliberate glance at Meg and Beth, then said to Cal, "The rest of us should go with you. You know the house best, but we can't be too careful."

Safety in numbers. Meg nodded that she understood. Beth grasped her hand harshly, afraid if she let go she was going to lose her.

"This way," Cal said, and disappeared into a hallway next to him; the darkness just welcomed him in and swallowed him up. There, and then gone.

Meg squeezed Beth's hand harder, a lifeline in the dark, and they followed him.

Every other time they had moved through the house the lights had been off and everything had been still, but this time, somehow, Meg felt everything much more acutely. Maybe it was the storm, crashing against the outside walls but still muted like it was happening on another plane of existence. Maybe it was the lack of the electricity humming, which meant there wasn't even the option of chasing away the dark. Maybe it was the flashlight Cal held in front of him, low enough that it didn't illuminate his face at all, so that it felt more like they were being led by a faceless ghost into the depths.

No. It was the memory of the floorboards caving in beneath her feet, the cords wrapping around her throat, drowning in the middle of dry land. It had felt personal. Malevolent. Old. And now she was putting herself at its mercy.

Well, the house and a murderer who called it home. It was hard to decide which one should take more of her attention.

"This is creepy," Beth said out loud.

"Agreed," Kendra said. She was sticking very close to Jay, enough to reach out to him if need be, but far enough away that it seemed they were blocking the hallway behind Cal. They were in front of Meg and Beth and behind Cal, she realized in the next breath: keeping them separate from him, where they would be safer. Kendra was a professional, and right now, in light of everything, she appreciated it, the reminder that they weren't alone.

"Don't worry. It's been through worse storms than this." But Cal kept glancing back and forth in the narrow hallway, on his guard against something. If it wasn't the storm, then she didn't know what it was. "We'll just wait it out like we always have."

"I don't know," Beth said. "It was falling apart when the wind wasn't sixty miles an hour outside."

Cal glanced over his shoulder, but didn't have a reply. It wasn't like she was wrong.

"Where's the breaker at?" Jay asked. "We're on the second floor, right? Aren't those usually in the basement?"

Cal didn't reply. Just kept walking, peering at the walls. It didn't look like the darkness bothered him at all. If they hadn't been here, she would bet they wouldn't have even bothered to look for it.

For lack of another option, Meg took out her cell phone and used the light as a flashlight so that she could see her steps. If there was a visual clue that the house was going to fall apart beneath her again, she intended to see it this time.

"You might want to save your battery," Cal said at last, moving his own flashlight in sweeping circles in front of them. "We don't even know this is going to work once we find it. Best be prepared for a long night."

He might have been right, but just because he suggested it, Meg didn't turn it off. Cal shook his head but didn't push the issue.

"Find it?" Kendra repeated belatedly, coming to the same conclusion as Meg. "Do you not know where it is?"

"I have a vague idea," Cal admitted, and he stopped and looked around them. "I haven't had to use it in a while, but I know it's on this floor. I think it's in here."

Meg looked around, too. This wasn't a hallway anymore: one of the hallways had ended in a great room of sorts, full of sheet-covered couches and chairs and end tables. The only thing not covered was a grandfather clock, carved of wood so dark brown it was nearly black and over six feet tall. Meg got the feeling if she went and stood next to it, it would dwarf her, so it was probably closer to eight. It didn't tick the way clocks were supposed to, though; all Meg felt was more silence, pressing, more immediate than the muffled storm beating against the walls outside.

Cal walked toward it, flashlight moving over the walls, and the rest of them spread out, too. Meg could barely see anything at all in the inky blackness, and it was difficult to move. The sheets that covered all the furniture were viscous as spider webs, and they moved at the slightest touch and tried to trap her ankles with each step. And there was no sign of the breaker.

"Anything?" Beth called from a few feet away.

Meg shook her head and looked around. Everyone else was shaking their heads, too, and Kendra sighed and put her hands on her hips. "Cal, I don't think it's in—"

There was an abrasive crash, and the grandfather clock fell to the ground on top of Jay.

Kendra's sentence curved up into a scream, high and short, and when she stopped the dust was still rattling from the walls and the air was still ringing, and Jay wasn't screaming the way she had.

Jay was silent. And still.

Cal stood next to it. No one else. He stared down at it with the same far-off look in his eyes from when he held Meg's hand over the cliff, like he wasn't the one making his own decisions, and there was no shock. No anger. No emotion at all. Just flat, glassy, growing brighter with muted horror as he came back into himself.

Jay wasn't moving. His head was turned unnaturally far to the side, and his eyes were still open.

Everything was becoming clearer. Brighter. Like dunking her head in ice water and then opening her eyes straight to the sun. Meg felt every inch of her skin like it was on fire, every thought in her head as it clanged and clambered for attention, the memory of danger in Cal's movements.

Murderer.

"I..." Cal said, still very calm, still muted horror in his eyes but no responsibility, and looked up at Kendra, who was as still as stone beside Meg. "I'm sorry."

Kendra opened her mouth and roared like an animal in a fight for its life and lunged for him.

Meg grabbed Beth's hand and ran.

Chapter Eighteen

eg clung to Beth's hand for stability and focused on the path in front
of their feet. One step after another. It was difficult to run when she
thought of how easily the floor had opened up and swallowed her before, but
she had to keep going. She had to get distance between them, quickly, before
Cal went after them too.

Because he would. She should never have thought for a second that he
wouldn't.

You knew this was coming, she told herself between the drumbeats of her
heart. *You had to know. You should have been ready.*

She hadn't. Now they were playing catch-up when Cal was steps ahead of
them and Jay was dead.

"Meg, if you don't say something, I'm going to start panicking," Beth said,
and her voice was very, very tight.

"We need..." And then she skidded to a stop in the middle of the floor. What
did they need? They couldn't call the police. They couldn't go to a neighbor.
They couldn't leave if they got to her car. They couldn't go into the forest.
Where? Why the hell hadn't she thought of an escape plan, in case they weren't
as protected by the others as she had assumed?

"The roof," Beth said at last, urgently, and turned to grasp her with both
hands on her shoulders. "If we get up there, maybe we can get a signal. Call
somebody. How do we get to the roof?"

"Why are you asking *me?*"

"The videos! Did they ever go up to the roof?"

Meg wracked her brain frantically. They had. She had even watched them get up there, once, and she remembered just a faint flickering.

"Does your dad know we're up here?"

"He doesn't know half of what I do in this house. Come on. Up here."

"Oh my gosh. Oh my gosh. Why do we have to come up here?!"

"Trust me, I have something to show you—a hiding place, if you will. Just hold on and don't look down."

Meg swallowed down her fear. To get to the roof...

"Is there or not?" Beth demanded.

"There is, but you're not going to like it."

"I *already* don't like it," Beth hissed, towing her around the corner by the elbow. Meg held her breath, listening for footsteps, for doors opening, for blood hitting the floor, but it was silent. Like they were alone. It made it that much worse. "Lead the way."

Meg took off running so she didn't lose her nerve, focusing on the hallways. It was so odd, but she did already know where to go. She did know these hallways; her feet followed the stairs and up and up like she was following a path glowing in the dark. She knew because she had followed Cal and Eliza up here over and over again. She hadn't known how crucial it was to watch the videos, but now they were both the reason they were running and the reason they were still alive.

So if she was wrong...

No pressure.

She ran faster, aware their every step rang through the entire house so speed was all they had. It felt like trying to outrun a shot arrow. She couldn't go fast enough.

No. Focus. Get to the roof, and he can't reach us.

"He doesn't know, does he?" Beth asked in a harsh whisper from behind her.

Meg skidded around the corner. "Know what? Where we are?"

"No—" Beth coughed, harsh and loud even though she tried to muffle it; Meg almost slowed down, but her legs didn't get the message and she was just relieved to hear Beth still behind her. They couldn't stop. "No. How we know."

"I... don't know. I mean, I don't know how he couldn't suspect, with how much I've been using from them—"

"But he doesn't *know* about them," Beth insisted. She was desperate, Meg realized, for any edge they could get.

And yes, that may have been the only one they had left. Cal didn't know how much Meg knew: about him, or his house, or what he had done.

"No," she said. "But I don't know how long until he figures it out."

It wasn't much, but for now, that meant he might not look for them on the roof. So that was the best plan they had.

"Alright." Meg stopped to catch her breath. They could only afford a few seconds, but if she didn't, her heart was going to beat right out of her chest. "It should be somewhere around—"

Beth lunged and put a hand over her mouth, expression wild and urgent; her heart kicked against her ribs and she froze. She heard something. Footsteps.

Meg looked all around, but there were no doors that she recognized. She didn't hear anything, so she didn't know which way he would be coming from, which way was safe and which was running straight into him and his dead eyes...

Someone rounded the corner in front of them, and Meg both tried to run and tried to lunge but in the moment that her body froze in indecision he jerked backwards in surprise, too, swearing under his breath.

Meg managed to pry Beth's hand off of her mouth. "Oh my god," she said, still shaking, "Bill. You're okay. I—I didn't—"

"A tree fell in front of the shed, so I came back to find something to try to move it." His eyes were so wide she could see white all the way around his pupils. Water dripped from his sleeves onto the floor. "What in the world's going on? I think I lost Mr. Arud and I don't know where Cal or the others are—"

"We're staying away from them," Beth said. "Fuck them, okay? They're fucking *crazy*. Cal killed Jay."

Bill's legs locked in shock and Meg shoved him the rest of the way into the room while Beth shut the door—but there was another door behind them. They couldn't hide in a room with more than one entrance. "Beth," she said urgently. "Come on. Keep going. Not here."

"*What?*" Bill said, like there was a delay on his brain. "How—why? Who?"

"Cal killed him," Beth spat, trying the door. "Why the hell are some of these locked—he killed him. He's a murderer. He killed Jay and Kendra attacked him but we haven't heard from Kendra in a while so she might be dead too. He's fucking *insane*."

If it was locked, they had to keep moving. To her surprise, though, Bill shouldered in front of them. "Give me a second, here. Let me try."

"Try *what?* It's locked!" Beth snapped. But Bill just dug in his pocket and pulled out a handful of keys. Some old, some new, a couple with dirt on them—none of them the car keys that he would have brought with them, and another tiny piece of the weekend slid into place.

"That's why you were snooping around the downstairs yesterday," Meg said. "You were trying a bunch of keys that you stole?"

"Borrowed," Bill muttered, and on the fourth key the door swung open. "Didn't think it would lead me here, for sure, but come on in."

Under the circumstances, it felt as close to a blessing as they were going to get. This door led to a smaller room, but it had only one door so it felt safe enough. Once they were all inside, Bill slammed the door shut, and they backed away from it. Meg braced herself for something to leap out of the dark, but nothing moved. Of course not. The only dangerous thing in this house was Cal, and he couldn't go through solid walls.

"There's something in this house," Bill said. Instead of terror in his voice, though, like Meg thought—expected—it was serenity. *Acceptance.* Borderline reverence.

"The only 'thing' in this house is Cal," Beth said, and threw her entire body weight against the bookcase next to the door; it fell to the ground with a resounding bang that shook in Meg's bones. *He'll hear,* that primal part of her thought, but the door was blocked so it wouldn't matter anyways. "And he's a devil, but he's human."

Bill didn't reply, looking over his shoulder into the dark behind them. There were no doors, Meg had already checked, but she found herself looking, too. It was instinct.

"You need to have more respect for the unknown than that," he said in a low, calm murmur. "We're only beginning to scratch the surface of what goes on in the world, you know."

"Did you not hear me? He killed people!" Beth glared at him. "And you have enough respect to steal keys and snoop around!"

"It saved us," Meg pointed out. And she didn't want to know, she didn't want to encourage him, she wanted them all to stop talking because the bookcase blocking the door didn't help her nerves at all, but... "Have you ever... you know, seen anything?"

"I've seen a lot of things you can't explain, Meg. That's why I spend my life looking for them. You get... addicted to it, almost. To this feeling that you're involved in something bigger than yourself, out of your depth, at the mercy of something other and mysterious and exclusive. It's a rush." He paused for a second, then said regretfully, "I love that rush."

Meg knew what he was talking about—but she had felt it just chasing after a human murderer. The kind of others he was talking about... if they existed, they weren't forces she wanted to mess with. She just wanted Cal to face justice for what he did. That was all.

It had felt so simple before this. Before what she was just realizing.

"Meg," Beth said in a harsh whisper. "Don't tell me you believe him!"

"You said it yourself: chandeliers don't just fall. And floors don't just collapse." She spun around, looking at the pieces of furniture littering the room.

This room was mostly tables, beautiful oak tables a shade lighter than they should have been with dust. It aged the room, turned it into a museum instead of a place people lived, and the white sheets moved in a nonexistent breeze... and it all seemed so alive. Something was watching her that she couldn't name. That couldn't be Cal. "And... I don't know. There are so many places where it seems like... like he's half-asleep and waking up in the middle of a sentence."

"Then he's crazy!" Beth hissed, but her eyes were stretched wide and her voice was shaking. "Not *possessed!*"

"I didn't say possessed. I just... don't think he's always in control of his actions," Meg said carefully. Not an excuse. Just an explanation. It was still murder.

"Yeah." Beth snorted, turning back to the door. "Real convenient, that he's not in control of himself when he kills people in front of us."

"That's exactly why it makes sense," Bill said, "Why would he do that with four witnesses?"

"Because we're still running from him like trapped rats!"

"It doesn't matter," Meg interrupted. They both turned to look at her, and she swallowed, hard, forcing her voice calm. "We need a plan. We can't just stay here. He'll find a way in eventually."

She found herself looking at Bill before she could stop herself—Beth was too—but he didn't look confident. There was some part of her, she realized, that hoped that since Bill was a man he would say that he could protect them if Cal found them. He was tall, and he looked stronger than she was at least... but he didn't volunteer that he would be any use in an actual fight. Kendra was a police officer, after all, and that hadn't saved her either.

The problem was, Meg thought with a shudder, that they didn't know what they were fighting. You could fight a person—but not someone unhinged, and between the chandelier and the floorboards collapsing, she wasn't sure that Bill wasn't right about the house.

"How long before people would come looking for us?" Bill asked quietly.

"Not until morning, at least. Afternoon? I... don't know who Kendra and Jay told." Just saying their names sent a pang of bitter sorrow through her. She could still see Jay's vacant expression, slightly bloody on the edges, staring up at her with accusation.

Not my fault, she told herself, *they were here anyways. I just elevated the stakes. I didn't fire the gun.*

"That's hours away. It's not even midnight." Beth glanced at the door like she had just realized, too, that they couldn't rely on that to protect them. And they hadn't heard footsteps or anyone trying the door, yet, even though they had set off an alarm as to where they had hidden. It didn't bode well at all. And Cal knew the house well enough to find them anywhere. A volatile, dangerous house.

"Can we get out? Into the forest?" Beth asked.

Bill shook his head. "The trees are all falling out there. It's a death trap," he said regretfully. "Especially since we don't know where we're going. What about the beach?"

"The tide's in. There's no beach to walk on, and I think if we try swimming we'll just kill ourselves," Meg said. "Even if we could get down those steps in the rain."

Beth threw her arms up in the air and started to pace in a circle, threading her hands through her hair. "Then... Then we just need to hide."

"It's his property," Bill said quietly. "We've only been here two days. Even with the keys I, uh... borrowed, there's no way we've seen everything."

Beth glanced at Meg in a swift, silent warning not to tell Bill about their conversation. The videos were going to be their secret. People who were desperate did stupid things, and Bill was still an unknown, a wild card. They couldn't risk their edge by telling him.

Beth whispered, "There has to be something—"

The floor outside the door creaked, and all of them froze. Not that it would help. Meg knew they would be found; she just hadn't expected it to be so soon. Not before they had thought of a plan.

The handle moved. Twisted. Back and forth. Back and forth. Not rattling. Calm.

The fear, already so heightened, doubled, hit her so hard and suddenly it felt like a punch in the gut. Before, she had been glad she wasn't alone; now, if he had a knife, if he had something they didn't know about, if he was something more than human, it helped nothing.

"Options," Beth hissed, "*Now.*"

"Nothing to use as a weapon," Bill said, hands shoved into his pockets as if he could have something he had forgotten about, and Meg looked around too. Anything, anything—but the furniture was too heavy, there were no windows or mirrors to break, there was nothing to swing. *Nothing.*

The lock clicked, quiet but full of magnitude, and Cal opened the door. The bookcase moved—just a fraction of an inch, but it moved. It wasn't going to hold. There was nothing heavier they could push in the way. Bill moved in front of them but he was shaking, he was out of shape, and they had *no weapons.*

"The roof," Beth said, "We're going there."

"What is there on the roof?" Bill demanded in a harsh whisper. "We'd just be trapped again!"

"He doesn't have a gun, so he might not reach us."

"You *assume* he doesn't have a gun!"

Meg swallowed. The roof was one of the only places that only had one entrance they could watch, and maybe he couldn't get up there, but even in this room with no windows she could hear the wind outside, ripping around the corners and peeling off the paint, and the rain pounding down on the roof was like dull thunder. Maybe she was hearing thunder. Maybe there was lightning and they would just make themselves lightning rods in the storm.

But she couldn't think of anything else.

"The roof," she agreed, "But how do we get out?"

"This way," someone said from the dark.

Meg shrieked and spun around, her heart in her throat. Had he—?

No. It wasn't Cal, it was the housekeeper, and he had appeared in what Meg had thought was a solid wall. He held open a panel, a pale smudge against the black void behind him. She hadn't heard him open it. She hadn't known it was there.

Bill breathed out harshly. "What kind of house is this?" he demanded.

Beth leaned over to Meg. "Do we trust him?"

There was no way to know for sure, but she nodded. He had warned her whenever she ran across him before, and that had to mean he wanted them alive.

"This way," the housekeeper said again, voice rasping. There was more life in his eyes than any other time Meg had seen him. Like he could see them this time. Like he was awake at last.

Cal tried the door again, and the bookshelf shoved back another inch. The crack of dim light widened and nearly reached them, sharp enough to saw them in half.

There were no other choices. None.

"Go," she whispered desperately, reaching for Beth's hand, and they followed the blind man down the tunnel that swallowed them up.

CHAPTER NINETEEN

The only way to get to the roof was to go out through the window.

Meg tried not to think that far ahead as she walked down the narrow corridor; there were only so many of her fears she could entertain at once before her body shut down and refused to move at all. Right now, it was the walls pressing in on her, and the ceiling low and scraping her head, so she just focused on the hunched back of the housekeeper in front of her and breathed through her mouth. The tang of dried wood and damp books was strong and thick, so she resorted to holding her breath. Almost there, almost there, almost there…

"What is this even for?" Beth whispered, voice tight like she was trying not to breathe either.

"Servant's entrance." Like it was obvious. Like all houses had secret tunnels. "Faster."

Something terrible occurred to Meg, enough she had to force her feet to keep moving. A few more inches with each step, closer, closer. "He knows about this, too, doesn't he?"

"He knows everything. Hurry."

He knows this house better than anyone alive. Faster. Faster. The walls pressed in and she couldn't outrun it so she squeezed her eyes shut.

She felt it when they reached the next room because her head didn't brush the ceiling anymore, but the air didn't change. It remained stifling, sticking in her throat like she was breathing in syrup, musty as death. When she dared look again, they were in a room like all the others, full of old furniture in beautiful colors—much of it broken—and the walls a shade of white that was five decades past clean. She had hoped for light, for blue, for anything that took the edge off the dark, but it all had the same look and feel: not just a show of a house that creaked and hid ghosts, but a house that belonged to a family living in shadow.

Whether the house was 'haunted' or not, the people here lived in the dark. Apparently that included their housekeeper, who had clearly been here for a very, very long time.

"You shouldn't have come here," he said.

"*You* brought us here!" Beth started, but Bill shushed her.

"He means the house," he said, talking slowly. As if that would help calm them down, with everything else going on. "Right?"

He was blind, it shouldn't have felt like anything, but Meg knew he was looking at her. "Why not?" she asked.

"You bring bad memories," he said, and for a second there was a deep understanding in his gaze. "You're speaking her words."

Meg's stomach flipped. He knew. "What happened to her?" she whispered.

"He killed her." He moved toward the door, softly, without purpose. Just to move, like he could pace ahead of the memories. "Killed her. The house shook with it."

"Oh my god," Bill muttered. "Kendra?"

"His fiancée," Meg said, feeling dazed. Here it was, the complete answer, the truth, the witness that would confirm everything she had thought—and it didn't matter at all, anymore. She felt like collapsing, but there was no time for that. "He pushed her off the cliff and killed her. Why?"

He didn't answer. Meg couldn't read his eyes. Regret? Maybe regret long accepted and shaped into something easier to handle.

No. He was waiting for her to figure it out, and she wracked her brain. If he was telling the truth and there was something making Cal act, what would it want? What was consistent across the stories that they had told them? What had she said over and over again, and it had triggered something she couldn't control?

He wasn't setting her free; he was leaving her alone.

The world is a lot bigger than your house, Cal. I can't believe you haven't seen it.

"She wanted him to leave," Meg said. "Didn't she?"

He didn't move, but slowly, a smile pulled at the edges of his lips. Spread wider, until he looked genuinely *happy*, but the expression in his eyes didn't change so it looked like a performance gone wrong. Meg shuddered and backed up a step so she was next to Beth, who held onto her hand and looked like she wanted to scream, but they didn't move. There was nowhere to go.

"You shouldn't have come," he repeated, still with no inflection in his voice but that smile on his face. "It knows you want to take him away."

Meg clamped her mouth shut around an involuntary yelp, holding so tight to Beth's hand that she was sure she was leaving marks. Her hand went to her throat, feeling the burns outside of it. It had a different meaning, now.

It didn't feel like an accident, anymore.

"We don't believe in this crap," Beth muttered, as though trying to make herself believe it. "Just... Just help us. Please."

The smile slowly, with the same amount of effort it had taken to form it, turned back to a neutral line. He turned forward again, listened for a second to the rain on the roof above them, and then looked back at them. "That way." He motioned toward the door in front of them, already open. Through it, Meg recognized the hallway as the one from the video, the one she had been trying to find. So she was right. It wasn't comforting.

"Thank you," Meg whispered, "Thank you so much."

His lips pursed—as through he was trying to smile, again. He didn't manage it this time.

"You aren't doing this for Eliza," he murmured.

That sense shot through her again, that he could see right through her skull into her mind, and the urge to scream rose with it. Transparency was *weakness.* She couldn't succumb to the fury, to the helplessness, to the sense that she was going to drown herself trying to swim against the current.

She couldn't afford that right now. She steeled herself, set her jaw, and didn't acknowledge how all of them were staring at her, waiting.

I'm here for Eliza.

The housekeeper waited a moment more, trying to read her silence, and then turned away. "Keep running. You remind him... of better times. The house wants you dead first, but he'll kill you last."

Meg's legs nearly buckled under her at the raw fear that swept over her. All that kept her from collapsing was Beth, who put an arm around her protectively with a level glare at him. "That's not comforting."

"The truth rarely is," he replied, looking at Bill for a second, then—"You'll die first. You believe."

Bill paled and swayed like he was going to pass out.

"We should go," Beth whispered, "Now."

Beth towed Meg by the hand, but she turned around to face the servant. "Thank you," she said, just because she had a feeling she wasn't going to see him again. "For your help."

He nodded back at her, face blank and resigned, as a crack of lightning lit his face and then threw it back into shadow. Just another part of the house once more. Another ghost.

"Run," he said.

Chapter Twenty

Beth and Bill followed Meg in silence down the hallway, trusting that she knew the way. She pushed herself to go faster, choosing speed over silence, every empty room and hallway on either side of them a dangerous unknown, and tried to think of something else they could do. Somewhere else they could go. Anything. There had to be something better.

But if there was, she couldn't think of it. The storm was going to get worse, and if they were going to call or signal to someone it would have to be from up there and it would have to be now.

"Here," Meg said, stopping short. She recognized that this was the right window, somehow. The trim around the edge of the glass. It was peeling more than anywhere else. It could be pried out more easily—and, more importantly, more quietly than the others on the floor. Cal had been so proud to show it to Eliza. *This is my secret way up to look at the stars.*

She tried the edges, and the pane of glass came out in one sheet. As soon as it did, the cacophony outside notched up in volume, no longer muffled, no longer something she could ignore: the wind howling, the rain pounding down in sheets, the branches snapping like bones as they hit the side of the house.

Bill laughed harshly. "You're fucking kidding me," he said. "We're going out the window? In this storm?"

"We're running from a murderer in a possessed house and that's what you're concerned about?" Beth demanded, standing up on the window sill. "You can go last, if you're so scared. Meg, come on. You first."

"...Thanks," Meg said, feeling like she was going to start laughing because the alternative was screaming. But she stepped up anyways. She had to keep moving. If she stopped, she wasn't sure she could start again.

Carefully, she reached out into the storm; the rain drove into her bare arm in nearly a solid sheet, like needles, but she got a tentative handhold on the edge of the roof above. Now she had to hoist herself up, putting her feet on the edge of the windowsill... *Yes, keep going...*

"I don't mean to hurry you," Bill said from inside, voice raised to be heard over the wind but as quiet as he could manage, "But faster."

Meg squeezed her eyes shut—it was so far down to the ground, if she didn't die she at least wouldn't be able to run and that was the same thing—and gripped it more firmly with both hands, and pulled. Beth pushed up on her feet, and she swung herself up so that she was standing on the edge of the window and looking up the roof. It was littered with branches carried over by the wind, and the runoff from the storm came down the sloped side and nearly into her face, solid as a flood.

Cal had always gone first in the video, and pulled Eliza up after him, because the first person had to *climb*. Why had she brought them here? Why was she doing this in sandals and a dress and a hurricane?

Because you have to.

Meg took a deep breath, flexing her grip to make sure she wouldn't let go when it mattered, and pulled up, walking along the side of the house. Beth was saying something beneath her, but it was whipped away by the storm and she couldn't stop anyways. Another shuffle up, her calves burning, her stomach ripping in half, her arms shaking...

You want to live. She choked back a sob and the impulse to go back down. *You want to live.*

It wasn't much, but she curled up enough to move from gripping with her hands to gripping with her whole arms, pushing on her elbows, and she dug her teeth into her lip and crawled up on her stomach. *Finally.* She took a second to lay there, drenched, relishing the cold because it helped her to breathe, and then pulled her legs up and turned around. "I-I'm here."

Nothing. The storm was too loud. She raised her voice. "Beth!"

Beth stuck her head out, saw where she was, and her face twisted with fresh fear. Meg couldn't hear what she was saying, but if she was reading her lips correctly she was mumbling *"oh god oh god oh god."* Maybe praying. A lot.

"Don't look down."

"Thanks, that helps," Beth bit out, breathing deep. "Okay, okay, okay..."

In one movement, maybe before she lost her nerve, she stood up on the windowsill, turned around, and grabbed for Meg's outstretched hand. Her skin was slick with rainwater, and Meg gripped tight enough to break her hand. She couldn't drop her. Couldn't.

"On three," she said, keeping her voice calm. Panic was contagious. They couldn't afford it. "Okay. One, two..."

She pulled and Beth jumped at the same time; it was easier for her to get her top half up onto the roof, leaning on her elbows, and Meg pulled her up and away from the edge as hard as she could. Beth rolled over onto her back, chest heaving, more adrenaline than actual exhaustion. "So, can you see anything?"

"I haven't looked yet." Meg leaned back over the edge, trying not to focus on the ground. It felt very easy to slip sideways, off, with the torrent of water rushing past her knees and sweeping the edges of her dress. "Bill!"

He looked out the window this time, up at them, and then down towards the ground.

"Don't!" Meg yelled, too late, as he blanched and swung back inside. Reconsidering. They didn't have time for hesitation. "Just come up! We'll help you!"

If we're strong enough, she realized with a sinking feeling in her gut. Bill was taller than either of them, heavier... but they didn't have a choice. She and Beth were already up here, and they needed to stick together. He needed to come up with them.

"Hurry," Beth hissed, reaching out her hand, "Hurry!"

Bill took a deep breath, muttered something that could only be a curse under his breath, and climbed up into the windowsill. He was tall enough that he could bypass Meg and Beth's hands and go straight for the edge of the roof, so he jumped.

And the edge cracked off in his hands.

It was just like in the video. There wasn't even time for him to scream.

Bill was falling one second, fallen the next. And Meg knew she was screaming but she couldn't make enough noise to drown out the sound she knew was coming. Nothing could. Everything had gone silent behind the roaring in her ears.

She didn't hear his head crack, but she knew the sound. Profound, but so simple at the same time. Like a tree branch that she broke for kindling against her knee when they were camping. Like a spark on a campfire. Like the crack of a whip against the air.

She shouldn't have heard it over the rain and wind, but she did, and when his head didn't break open against the ground she held her breath. She heard it, but... but...

Is it wrong to hope someone is dead?

Beth clutched her hand, muttering something under her breath that Meg couldn't make out. She was going to pass out. She was going to fall and break her own neck and that was the only thing that kept her only swaying and not falling, too.

The front door opened, and Cal walked out.

A pang of bittersweet anger rushed through her, so strong she snarled with it. He hadn't even been right behind them; there had been no need to hurry. It had only been this damn cursed house, breaking apart underneath them because it didn't want them here.

Meg breathed in sharply when he leaned down to Bill's body—Bill? Was he dead? There were worse things than death, she realized now, her veins gone cold with horror.

Cal straightened. He was blocking Bill's face. All Meg could do was hope he was dead. Hope that Cal had enough humanity left in him to be merciful and kill him if the fall hadn't.

He turned around and looked up at them. Beth held her in a vice grip, and Meg knew she stood out clearly to him, a beacon in the storm, her white dress waving in the wind. There wasn't anything to hide behind. He knew where they were. He knew the house. He could get up here just as well as they could. It had all been a fool's hope.

Thunder boomed, and half a second later lightning lit them all up like the flash of a camera, so close and immediate Meg felt all the hair on her arms stand on end with the charge.

It illuminated Cal's face as he held up a key that had been on Bill's body. It was bigger than the other keys, more ornate, and rusted from use in the weather—which meant it was the one that led to the outside gate. To freedom.

He was smiling, content. Meg read it as perfectly as if his lips were forming the words.

I have the only key.

CHAPTER TWENTY-ONE

Meg stared down at Bill's body, unmoving, face sunken in the mud deep enough that if he only had a broken neck he would have drowned by now, and thought at herself, *move. You have to move. You can come up with a new plan of attack or escape later but right now you have to **move.***

She couldn't. The rain pelted into her skin like tiny shards of glass, and the wind lifted her hair so that the burns on her neck felt fresh and raw again, and her dress was soaked through and dripping off of her onto the sodden roof, and Bill was dead and Cal was coming for them next.

Move. Move. Move!

"Meg," Beth said, her voice quiet and breaking, barely heard over the wind, "There's no one we can signal to."

Of course—the reason they were here in the first place. She raised her eyes, already sure of what she was going to see in front of her: nothing. No lights on the horizon. No boats out in the turbulent sea. No houses close enough that they would see two people waving on the roof or even a light. And Beth had taken her phone out, to see if she had any bars, but it still had no signal. Meg's own phone had finally died, the battery drained, and she stared at the black screen and clicked the button automatically but nothing changed.

They were alone. Completely alone, and there was no way they could call for help.

Meg breathed out through her mouth. "Useless," she whispered. All of it. And now they had to *get back down.*

"Do we think it's worth staying up here?" Beth asked.

"No. There's probably another way up here we don't know about, and then there'll be nowhere to run." That had to be the secret behind how slowly Cal walked back into the house. There had to be something they were missing. They weren't two steps in front of him, they were ten behind.

"Then how do we get down?" Beth asked, voice shaking. "Because we don't exactly have a ladder."

Meg closed her eyes, focusing, and found the strength to stand up even though her legs felt brittle enough to crack under her. Realistically, this house was a maze. Realistically, there had to be another way up here that was more practical and not the romanticized way of a boy trying to impress a girl. It hadn't been in the videos because that wasn't the way he had gone, but...

She moved slowly, studying the roofing at her feet, and finally saw one of the pieces that didn't align with the next. She reached down and tugged on it, and when she put all her strength into it, they were looking down into the house again.

A trapdoor. It led down into darkness, much shallower than the hallways of the house they had been through so far, that had to be an attic. That made sense.

She glanced behind her at Beth, who looked ashen. "I wish I'd known about this before," Meg said, but it fell flat. Humor felt sacrilegious standing over a dead body.

Beth swallowed hard. "How do you know about it *now?*"

The look in her eyes was terrible, so Meg looked down again instead. "I don't know. I've stopped asking that question. Come on."

Beth didn't say anything when Meg disappeared back down into the house, and she was slow to follow.

The attic had a different feel to it than the rest of rooms in this house. People went in the other rooms just often enough—the housekeeper to dust, Cal and his father to do whatever they did—that they felt, on the surface, lived in. Or at least livable. The attic, though, felt much like the basement had: barren, and the air thick like something more than dust had settled here, and old enough that anything could happen.

Meg didn't mean to stop, once they made the short jump down and shut the entrance behind them, but her legs gave out; she shivered hard enough her bones felt brittle, could shatter if she moved too fast. Her skin felt sliced open, and she rubbed her icy, sodden arms and looked down at the ground. Her dress was dripping, in a wide circle around her feet, breaking through the thick carpet of dust in an uneven pattern.

"We need to go," Beth whispered.

Meg just shook her head, her teeth chattering too hard to speak. She couldn't. Not when she couldn't even feel her legs.

She waited for Beth to insist, but she just sighed heavily and sank down next to her. She was shivering, too, but the warmth of her arms against Meg's still helped her to shake less. Meg clenched her teeth together to mute the sound of them clacking together. All noise was dangerous, and she had to warm up fast so they could run again.

Again. Somewhere new. She had no idea where.

"It wasn't supposed to be like this," Meg said. Her voice came out smaller than she had hoped, and shakier. That wasn't going to reassure Beth.

"No," Beth agreed, "No, it definitely wasn't. Although if it helps, I don't think Cal intended for this to happen either. I don't think my waiver says my family won't sue if I die."

Meg laughed for her, but it mixed with a sob. Beth put her hand in her hair, her own attempt at comfort, and Meg closed her eyes and listened to her heartbeat: fast, but steady, and sure. Something grounding in the dark that reached out to get her.

"We shouldn't have come here," Meg whispered.

"No," Beth agreed again, and that was all there was to say to that. It was already done, and all the damage along with it.

That didn't absolve her of anything, though. She hadn't realized the magnitude of what she was getting into. She hadn't known Eliza; it had been about the chase. It had been a thrill, an adrenaline rush like Bill was seeking when he searched for the unexplainable, something she could chase when she had been directionless for so much of her life. He was a murderer, yes, there were high stakes, yes, but she was protected because she was too good to get caught. Because he didn't want to kill her, she had been sure.

And now. Now the force of how wrong she was, how *naïve* she had been... the guilt of it was physically suffocating.

Stupid. Stupid, stupid, stupid, **stupid.**

She thought she was being so careful, and now Beth and her were the only ones alive. The only ones left out of *five.*

"Any ideas?" she asked Beth in a whisper.

"I'm not sure you want more of my ideas. My last one was the roof." Beth paused; her hand tightened in Meg's, just barely, and her face crumpled, on the edge of tears but unable to spare the energy for it.

"Stop that," Meg ordered. "If you want to play the blame game right now, I was the one who brought us here."

"I was the one who didn't believe you." Beth looked up at the ceiling. Maybe listening to the wind crashing against the side of the house. It sounded like an animal—another thing trying to kill them. "If it helps, I believe you now."

"I should hope so." She wondered, abstractly, if Bill or Kendra or Jay had family that was waiting for them to come home from this with nothing but stories. She hadn't bothered to learn anything about them except the basics, what a polite but disinterested stranger would ask; she had been too wrapped up in Cal and proving what he was. Was Bill married? Did Kendra and Jay have children? Did they have things they wanted to do that they couldn't anymore?

Stop. She had to stop. This wasn't going to help them. It wasn't going to bring anyone back.

"What's the plan?" she asked. She was better with a direction, with something to focus her thoughts on besides mindless panic. She just had to get started and the rest would follow.

Sure enough, Beth took a deep breath and got to her feet abruptly enough Meg listed sideways and had to catch herself on an elbow. It brought a somewhat smile to Beth's face, a lighter look to her eyes that suited her better.

"We get moving," she said, pulling Meg up with her. "Any more tricks up your sleeve from...?"

"Not right now," Meg admitted. She had a few more videos of the house that she had watched, but technically the roof had been her idea.

Beth froze suddenly, head tilted slightly to the left, listening. She had to hear something Meg hadn't noticed—and sure enough she grabbed for Meg's hand and dragged them both toward the trapdoor that led down to the rest of the house.

Of course. They needed to move, now, because this was the only place Cal was going to think to look for them from the roof. And her dress was still damp, she still felt as icy cold from skin to bone as before, but she could move. And they had to, so she would.

The door led down into another great room, like the one Kendra and Jay had died in (don't think about it, don't think about it), and there was no ladder so they just dropped down into the middle of it. The drop collapsed Meg's knees under her, shocks of pain all up her legs and her back that she bit down on her lip to keep quiet against, and when she got back up there was a huge, impossible-to-miss imprint in the dust.

So they couldn't hide here.

She moved a chair over for Beth to step down onto and looked around. Nothing in this room but low couches, low end tables, low chairs, and a few boxes. Nothing to hide behind. Nothing to use as a weapon. There was nothing useful in this whole house.

"Thanks," Beth said, moving it off to the side. "Now we—"

She froze; Meg already had. It was instinct, deeper than she could explain, something that plucked at her nerves one after another after another.

Run, that voice whispered with increasing frequency. *Run. Run. Run. Run or die.*

There was someone coming.

"Do you know where we're going?" Beth asked in a ragged whisper.

Meg couldn't spare the energy to actually say no so she just shook her head. No, she didn't know where she was going anymore. She couldn't draw on her memory of the videos through her adrenaline, or whatever weird sense she got that her logic was almost memory too, she was just running. They were ahead of Cal, but she didn't know for how much longer.

Eventually, they were going to run into him, and even though there were two of them and one of him, Meg still didn't like their odds.

"Plan?" Beth insisted.

"Get away from him. Find somewhere to hide until people come in the morning."

She was too afraid to consider the possibility that people might not come in the morning. They had to. Surely someone would think to check on them after a storm like this, if nothing else.

She hoped.

Beth yanked her hand to bring her to a sudden stop, listening, and pulled them down a different hallway.

"How can you hear him?" Meg hissed. She could barely hear anything at all over the rain falling heavy on the roof and the wind trying to tear the siding off and the branches hitting the windows.

"I'm pretty sure I'm delusional, but I'll take it at this point." Beth pulled them around another corner and into a room the size of their guest rooms, flattening herself against the wall and not closing the door. "I don't know where we can hide, though. Do you—"

"No." Meg coughed; her throat, still recovering from nearly suffocating yesterday night, felt as dry as if it were stuffed full of embers. And running wasn't helping. "Just don't stop."

Beth clutched her hand tighter and didn't bother to reply. They were going to have to stop eventually, was the problem. There was just where, and whether it cost them.

Maybe she was hallucinating too, but Meg pulled so that Beth swung around and took them in the opposite direction. There was no way she was actually hearing things, but she thought there was something in the hallway ahead of them. Footsteps, slow and measured and purposeful.

"Move," she whispered urgently, grabbing Beth and dragging her along with her down the hallway in the opposite direction. She didn't know where she was going and she didn't care anymore. Away. That was literally all she wanted anymore, to get away from Cal, even for a few more seconds.

Keep moving. If we stop, we die.

This voice in her head was terrible. Meg hated her. She just wanted to stop.

But they couldn't.

When they were on the opposite side of the house, though, Meg's lungs couldn't take any more. She nearly collapsed against the wall, but even though her legs shook she somehow managed to stay upright, holding Beth for support.

She listened so intensely that she felt her heart in every inch of skin, but she could hear nothing over the driving rain.

"We can't keep doing this," Beth said, voice breathless with fear, with the same realization, "We can't. We're not getting anywhere and there aren't any weapons and there's no one we can call for help—"

"We have to," Meg interrupted, trying to calm her back down. She had to focus her. Center her. They couldn't afford to lose themselves. Cal would win. "Okay? We can do this. There has to be something."

She ran her hands over the edge of the wall, ignoring how cold and dusty it was, feeling for indents. They hadn't seen the one that the housekeeper had come out of, before, but surely now that they knew about them there would be more.

"What are you doing?" Beth hissed.

"Finding a way out he doesn't know we can use," Meg whispered. She resisted the urge to shove things out of her way when there was furniture against the wall—too much noise, the whole point was to be quick and quiet in their escape—and kept running her fingers along the edge. "So we can... maybe hide. Maybe get a head start. Maybe find some of those things that I found the boxes for. I don't know, something."

"But he would know about these." But Beth helped her look, going into the next room, close enough for them to hear each other but cover more ground. "And why wouldn't he use a knife or a hammer if he had them?"

She didn't know, but she didn't want to find out. It took willpower to close her eyes, to let herself feel instead of look for the entrance they needed. There had to be one, in one of these rooms, and this one was big enough to hold it, and...

There. There was a raised edge on this panel, just next to an antique dresser covered in cobwebs and dust, and when she ran her fingers down it there was a tiny click before it pulled open. She laughed in exhilaration. "Beth!"

Beth laughed, too, coming next to her. "I don't believe it," she said, but there was an edge to her voice that Meg couldn't place. "You were right. How are you right?"

At this point, she didn't care. Meg shook her head and pulled it open. "Hurry. Before he finds us again."

But Beth didn't move. She looked at Meg and the passageway, and then back at the door, and hesitated. She had been scared, before, but now there was a bone-chilling certainty to it that stole her breath away.

"What?" Meg whispered.

Beth swallowed hard. "If you really want him not to know where you are," she said haltingly, "We should cover our tracks."

The dresser. Meg could see where she was going with this. The dresser was so covered in cobwebs that if it was in front of this entrance, Cal would assume they hadn't used it. Wherever they went, they would have time—to plan, to wait for help, whatever they needed.

But she saw no way to move it from inside the entrance.

Only from the outside.

There was only one way to do this, Meg thought with the one part of her that still functioned, and it was terrible but it was the *only way*. She felt sick to her stomach and weak in her bones but underneath, the purpose was strong and clear.

"We're splitting up," Beth breathed.

Meg stopped short, the words dying in her throat; the purpose, the strength, left her all at once with the force of recognition. That was supposed to be what *she* said. She was the one who had dragged them here, so she had a responsibility to get them out.

She had been scared before, but she was really terrified of the finality of the words in the dead air between them.

"So we have a better chance of getting out," Meg whispered.

That wasn't what Beth's face said when she gripped her wrist hard enough her nails dug in. "Listen to me," she said, and pressed something into her hand. It had the smooth, definite feel of a pocketknife. She must have smuggled it in where Meg hadn't thought they were in danger, always three steps ahead, always willing to do what she was afraid to. It took real effort to put it in her dress pocket so she couldn't accidentally drop it because her hands were shaking too hard to function.

"Listen to me," Beth repeated, her voice a touch rougher, and a tear leaked out of her eye and disappeared into her mouth, which was gritted into a snarl. "Don't stop running. And if he finds you, if he tries to hurt you, you kill him. Understand? *Kill him.*"

Alarm sparked in Meg's mind. "What—?"

"*Promise me,* Meg."

*Where's **your** knife?* She swallowed, hard. "You too," she managed finally. "You... kill him, too."

Beth grinned, a little wildly, breaking apart right in front of Meg's eyes. "This was your show from the start," she said. "You know that. And you know how to do it."

Because she had the dress. Because she had the videos. Because she had been playing this game, so if he was going to kill her, he was going to kill her last.

She would use it. She would use it to get Beth out, get them both out, no matter how much it scared her or how much it cost.

"Go," Beth whispered, but she couldn't let go of her hands even when she half-heartedly shoved her backwards. Towards the passage, towards safety. She was still crying. "Go!"

That wasn't a plan, but there wasn't time to argue with her.

Meg choked down a sob and tore herself away and ran.

She ducked inside, closing the door behind her, and hated herself for it.

She didn't want to, but she listened for sounds behind her, for what was happening to Beth or if anything was happening at all; now, when she needed it most, the sounds were completely lost behind the storm, which had picked up ferocity. Nothing. She might as well have been alone.

Think.

She moved through it and pressed on the panel on the other end, emerging this time into a hallway. She tried to place the layout of the house in her mind, tried to call up some semblance of control when everything was moving far too fast. Nothing was recognizable, not yet at least. She needed to find a way around, to get behind Cal when he got to where she and Beth had been, a few seconds from finding them. She had a knife. It was tiny but with the element of surprise...

She skidded to a stop.

That door was still closing, like it had just been opened, but she had run *away* from Beth and Cal which meant—

Something hit her in the back of the head, and she fell.

Chapter Twenty-Two

Even though she prayed for it, tried to make it happen, would have begged out loud for it if her lips would move, Meg didn't fall unconscious with the hit. Everything just went slow, sluggish, and sideways. Like being drunk. She could see but her vision was hazy, and her body wasn't responding but she felt it when she was dragged over the floorboards by her arms. Like she was already dead. Her dress caught against the floorboards in a few places but for the most part it was smooth beneath her legs.

It was cowardly, it was stupid, it wouldn't do anything, but she had hoped they would kill her and she wouldn't know it. She was hoping not to know, so that it would be quick. Like falling into a sleep that swallowed her the way the floor had. So that it would be over like it had been for Eliza. Simple. Fast. *Crack.* Done.

But he hadn't killed her. Was just dragging her like he was an animal, or she was, and there were tears running down her cheeks but she couldn't feel them. She couldn't see where they were going.

Don't let them drag it out, she thought, but...

He'll kill you last.

Did that mean she was going to wish he had killed her first?

She didn't want to think about it. There was nothing to do but think about it.

Let me wake up now, she thought. *Let me wake up and be at home or let me go to sleep now and not feel the shift into death.*

She closed her eyes again, feeling faint and terrified, and this time darkness was swift and complete.

She wasn't sure it counted as dreaming if you were unconscious, or if she even was unconscious, but there was a singular thought in Meg's mind. It wouldn't go away. It wouldn't shut up. It was a needle, a pin-prick pain that once it had broken the skin, once she let it in, got more and more intense, sharper, all-consuming.

You aren't doing this for Eliza.

The memories are terrible, and now, when she needs calm the most, they rear their ugly heads and she suffocates with the strength of them.

She's eight and she's clinging to Beth's hand because the adults are talking to her for the first time in six hours. They're not talking normally. They're using their 'you're-too-young-to-hear-this' voices that mean something terrible has happened and they have no choice but to be the bearers of bad news.

Meg already knows what it means, that they didn't come back with their friend Dinah. She's young, but she's not as naive as they seem to think she is. She knows about death. Her cat died last year. She didn't see it, she just knows it left and her parents came and kneeled down and spoke to her like they are now. They're not coming back. They're so sorry, honey.

Dinah's uncle is at the end of the hall, the one she came to Meg's house to avoid.

He goes into the bathroom and Meg sees blood on the back of his hand.

The world tunnels, but the adults think her screams are grief. They don't understand.

"So, Cal, all of the stories..." She pauses a second, thinking, looking at the walls around them. "Are they true?"

"You're going to have to be more specific." While she seems nervous, her voice low so that whatever they are talking about can't hear them, he sounds amused. They're stories, after all. And it is his house. "Which ones?"

She shrugs, still watching the hallway in front of them. It's a house that they're in, a house that people live in, but the hallway still looks abandoned, as though no one has set foot in it for decades. The darkness is calling, enticing, and the camera focuses down it for a moment even though there's nothing there.

As soon as it's clear it's empty, the focus shifts back to her. "There's nothing there."

"I know." She laughs, once, but it's not as carefree as it usually is. She knows, but she doesn't believe it. "But really. Are they true?"

"Which one?"

"I don't know... the one that says there's ghosts?"

"No ghosts." He pauses, focuses on her face when it starts to turn into a smile again. "Just us."

"Meg, hon—"

"I know I'm right, Mom! It was him! Her uncle!"

Meg is young but she can already feel the high of victory, so much that it drowns out the fury. Dinah might be dead, but the man who did it—she knows. She knows. Dinah might not be coming back, but Meg pays attention and she knows bad people should get what they deserve. And for taking Dinah, he deserves **everything.**

But Meg's mom and dad, Dinah's parents and family, Beth still shell-shocked because she hasn't even had a pet go somewhere and never come back... they don't look angry. They look sad.

Meg's conviction wavers.

"It wasn't him, Meg," her dad says, carefully, like there's something that she's not seeing, "And I know you think you're helping, but—"

"It was him!" she blurts. "I know it was!"

Beth gasps and reaches for her, finally starting to cry, and Meg gives her hand for her to cling to but she doesn't really feel it. She hasn't cried yet. Can't. The purpose...

"It wasn't anyone, Meg," Dinah's mom rasps. Her voice sounds broken, like a piece of her is physically missing. Meg has never seen an adult crumble like that. More than anything, even the blood, that is terrifying. "It was just an accident."

"But... But..." Why aren't they listening to her? "I know it was!"

Meg's mom shakes her head and turns to Dinah's parents, gentle and slow. "I'm so sorry..."

Beth cries harder, but Meg feels her heart harden, crystallize, into something stronger than steel. She doesn't join her.

There's a short yell; the camera had been filming the ballroom around them, but now it spins around jarringly fast. Behind, and then down to the floor, and then moving—he's forgotten it's on, he's just running. "Liz?"

"Over... Over here."

There's a brief clear image on the camera: of her lying on the floor on the edge of the ballroom, holding her leg. Her jeans have been torn open and there's blood underneath; the camera falls to the ground, catching only the edge of his knee and the side of her shirt when she sits up. "Oh my god—"

"I'm fine, I'm fine. I just... stepped wrong. The floor caved in under me."

He breathes out shakily. "Okay. Okay, um... Can you stand?"

"Yeah, just help me please—" The floor creaks when she shifts and they both freeze. Both waiting, trying to decide whether it's safe, and she breathes out. "That doesn't look like metal I cut myself on, right?"

"I don't think so." He shifts to look down into it. "You're good. Come on. I have bandages over here."

"I'm fine," she repeats. "Really. It was just an accident."

He lingers for a moment more, and then they move away, the camera forgotten and still recording on the floor.

*"Meg, you have to **stop.** "*

She doesn't know how to stop. She knows what she saw. That conviction hasn't wavered since that moment of clarity. It was Dinah's uncle. She's been giving him a wide berth. Whenever she gets too close to him, the shudders crawl all over her body like spiders. She knows all the way down to her bones what dangerous looks like now.

Meg looks up at Beth. She's crying again. She's done a lot of crying recently. Meg hasn't. She's been focused.

"It wasn't him," Beth spits, and Meg jolts; it's the first time she's seen her angry.

She feels like she's going to cry now, finally, but it has nothing to do with Dinah. "You don't believe me?"

"No!" Beth storms out. "And you're making it worse, so just... just drop it!"

The door slams behind her.

Meg stares down at the paper she was looking at, where she's written down the exact description of the blood she saw on the back of the man's hand right after they found... her body. It wasn't a normal cut on his hand. It was a scratch, like one she made when she was roughhousing with Beth and Dinah so long ago and yet still so close to the front of her memory. She remembers how she had nothing bad to say about anyone but she stayed away from her uncle, refused to be alone with him, asked to stay with them instead.

But they're not going to believe her. It's been two months and they're... moving on. Marking it off as an accident that she fell from an overpass walking home from school, because she liked to walk on the barrier instead of on solid ground and this time she made a mistake. Tragic, but nothing more. An accident. It takes the power away from it, to think there was no one behind it.

It loosens its hold.

That's all they want: to move on. To forget. And all she wants to do is help, but if she's hurting them and she should stop...

But she can't.

Dinah is gone. She's never going to laugh at one of her jokes again, she's never going to pet her cat again, she's never going to get the gift she and Beth picked out for her birthday. She's never going to grow up.

Her story is just... over. Ended mid-sentence, before she got to be the vet or horse trainer—she hadn't decided—or have a wedding or go to the horse-riding camp that only took high schoolers. It's all gone. There's nothing but 'wanted to be' and 'could have been.'

She can't forgive that.

She refuses.

They're sitting inside of his room. It's still barren, just as it has been in every video, but now there are a few more signs of life. A vase of flowers sits on the end table—roses from outside. The comforter on the bed is a very light blue. The room is free of dust.

She sits on the bed, smiling across at him. "What are you filming now? Are you proposing to me again?"

"You just look nice today. That's all."

"You charmer." She stands, stretching. She's wearing jeans again, and a shirt that looks like one of his. "You look nice too. Why don't I film you for a change?"

"I don't like myself on camera."

It takes a second before she rolls her eyes. "You're hilarious."

"I know. Thank you." He pauses, still following her as she leans against the windowsill and looks outside. It's sunny, and it illuminates the room so that, for the first time, it looks normal. "Really, I know myself. I want to have this to remember you by."

She smiles, shakes her head. "I'm not going anywhere."

"I know. But... I want to remember every second of it."

"Meg?"

She looks up from her work. She's reading about a journalist who went out after a corrupt businessman and found enough evidence to put them behind bars, in spite of how powerful they were. It makes her feel better, to read that it's possible. It keeps her going. She's having a hard time keeping focused.

She's starting to forget. What she saw. What she felt. All the things that Dinah did and all the things that were taken from her too soon. And it should feel like a good thing, to forget, for the emotions to lessen. It means healing, her mom says. Everyone stops crying over even the worst things after long enough.

It should be a good thing. But it doesn't feel like it. And she really doesn't want to talk to Beth, who gives her a side-eye every time she looks at her. She waits, but she doesn't expect much.

Beth hesitates. "I have something for you. Dinah gave it to me, but... I think you need it more."

She throws it, and Meg catches it. It's a stone—one that she recognizes immediately. It is a mottled gray-green with a white band around it; when she runs her fingers over it, the gray-green part is smooth and the white band is raised and *rough. There is a smooth indent in the middle, so that she can put her finger in the middle of it, like an old stone for pounding herbs in the book they had been reading in class. That must have been why Dinah had picked it up.*

She strokes her thumb in the indent, imagines Dinah doing the same. She knows where she found this. It was at the beach an hour away; they had gone there together a few months before the "accident." It had been so hot that day, so that the roads were full of shimmering imaginary puddles. She and Beth and Dinah ran up and down the beach for hours, the sun beating down relentlessly until her shoulders started to blister, jumping over the waves as they rolled in and collecting piles of different rocks and shells. It was a good day. When she thinks about it, she can smile. When she holds this stone in her hand, she can feel where Dinah held it, too.

It feels like she's here.

She doesn't have to forget. She remembers by having this, by having a piece of her life to hold onto and keep with her. If she keeps this, if she remembers the memory that goes with it, it's like she's not dead at all. She's not here, but... as long as she remembers her, this piece of her is alive.

It helps. It loosens the claws in her brain, makes it a little easier to breathe.

She hears Beth walking away, down the stairs, and makes the decision. She shoves the rock in her pocket—it's like she's still with them, her throat is tight but everything has to stop hurting eventually—and throws the book to the side.

She tries to forget.

Is anyone going to look for me when I'm dead?

When Meg woke up, her senses came back in groggy, unclear pieces, one after the other. She was still alive. She was breathing—faster, when she realized it, it was instinct to suck down as much as possible, knowing each inhale might be her last. She was sitting up, hands pulled behind her, in a stiff-backed chair.

She couldn't move.

"Meg?"

She jerked her head up, vision blurring with too much adrenaline and nowhere to place it, a cry building in her throat, and the person in front of her... put their hands up.

"It's alright," Cal said. "Just me."

They were in another basement; it felt the same as the one with the sandal and the crow, and had all the same marks, but it was too small. The same darkness all around them, so complete it would have been difficult to see Cal's face if he wasn't so close to her. The same musty smell, like this was somewhere they didn't go unless they had no other choice. It was eerily silent, the rain and wind very far away. The only sounds were the faint creaking and rattling of pipes under the house as it settled and her own fast, uneven breathing. A rat scratched at some wood in the dark, rhythmic and sharp in the quiet.

Meg sucked down another breath so she didn't scream because *it already felt like a tomb...*

"Hey! Hey." Cal still had his hands up, and he took a small step back so that his face was even less visible. "It's okay. It's just me. Take your time."

It was so bizarre that Meg laughed hoarsely. "Just you?" she repeated.

"Just me," he said again, as though he didn't understand the irony, and put his hands at his sides. He didn't make a move toward her, just stared, and his face was calm. Peaceful. There was no blood on it, or sign of the rain or mud. He could have put on his charming smile from the party and it wouldn't have been out of place. "How are you feeling?"

"Where's Beth?"

Nothing. Not a single twitch of his face. "Are you okay?" he asked. Like he was on fucking autopilot.

"Are you joking?" Meg demanded. Her throat was rough, though, and the words came out soft and raspy. It didn't match the emotions she wanted to put to them at all. "I'm tied to a chair!"

"I didn't think you'd listen to me otherwise," he said. "Are you willing to listen?"

Hysteria was building in the back of her mind, her instinct was to start screaming at him, but Meg swallowed with difficulty and forced it back. Forced herself to think. He apparently wanted to talk. Every second he talked was another second she lived. Another second closer to getting free, finding Beth, and getting out.

She could play this game, the same way she had played all the others: very, very carefully.

"I don't really feel like I have a choice," she said, because it would be unrealistic not to. "But... yes. I'll listen. Cal, what's going on? What's..."

What's wrong with you, she wanted to ask, but managed to stop herself. Cal seemed to understand what she was thinking, though, because he took a deep breath, readying himself for an explanation, seeming... almost nervous. How was this the same person she had just watched murder somebody a few hours ago?

"It's going to sound crazy," he said. "You're going to think I'm crazy."

It was very, very difficult to keep her voice level, her face calm, when every nerve in her body was screaming. This felt more dangerous than a maniacally laughing, screaming, blood-covered Cal like she had been expecting. This was someone holding it together when logic dictated they should be unhinged. "I think I'll believe anything at this point. Try me."

Another deep breath, and he glanced over his shoulder; Mr. Arud was there, Meg saw with a new rush of fear. She hadn't even noticed him, had nearly forgotten about him when he walked with a limp and seemed so ordinary—but he must have been the reason she heard someone when she was with Beth but had been ambushed from the opposite direction. He had his arms crossed, leaning against the wall in a corner, his suit crisp and dry. Had he taken the time to change after going outside before coming down to watch his son murder their guests?

His eyes moved between her and Cal, observing a train wreck already in progress, and Meg looked back at Cal before she could shudder. She had to focus. Her life depended on it.

"I... hear things," Cal said haltingly. "Something lives in the house. And it talks to me."

Meg laughed once before she could stop herself, heart in her throat. "Like a person?" she asked desperately.

He tilted his head. "Kind of? It's hard to explain. But it tells me... what I need to know. What I need to do. It always has."

Insane. That was the only word Meg could think of... and yet, the house felt ancient, and watchful, and vengeful. He hadn't made the chandelier fall, or the floor collapse beneath her, or the edge of the roof break off...

No. No, she couldn't think like that. That could have been terrible, dangerous luck. She couldn't believe like Bill, in things she couldn't see. She couldn't fight ghosts. Cal was bad enough. It was just so easy to forget that ghosts didn't exist down here, with the pipes rattling like bones and the darkness that breathed.

"That..." How did she go about this delicately? "Do you have any proof? Anything you can show me?"

"No," Cal said, holding his head high, as if it was something he was proud of. Like there was something else, something older, shadowing his stature. The same way the presence had breathed on the back of her neck in the basement with the crow. "But I feel it. I always have. It's a part of me. I hear the voices, in the house, and they help me. Make me... whole. I believe in it, and it makes me... more."

"Whether or not you believe something doesn't make it true," Meg breathed. A part of her wanted to raise her voice, but the hairpin trigger on Cal was so fine and clear she couldn't risk it. "Only crazy people think like that."

Cal laughed and threw his hands in the air. "Then I'm crazy!" he said helplessly. "Then I'm crazy. But the house talks to me. It always has. Just because no one else hears it doesn't mean I can't."

She was afraid to ask, she didn't want to ask, but... "What does it tell you?" she whispered.

His arms dropped to his sides, suddenly enough Meg flinched, and he looked at her sideways. A shark smelling blood in the water. How had he passed for normal for so long? "It told me you were coming," he said. "That you *knew me*, and you were coming anyways. And it was right. I knew the second I saw you standing in the same spot where Eliza died. I knew you were... what I needed."

"You mean where you killed her," Meg challenged. Her heart was hammering in her chest. She wanted to hear it. She wanted to see the look on his face.

But nothing changed in his eyes. No regret. No surprise, to hear her accuse him of murder. In fact, he blinked at her. "I don't... It was an accident."

"Don't bother," Meg snapped, the fury breaking free at long last. She had thought about throwing it in his face for too long. "I know it was you. I—" She stopped herself at the last second. She couldn't tell him about the videos. They were all she had left. "You pushed her off the cliff."

He raised an eyebrow and glanced over his shoulder at his dad, who shrugged; satisfied, Cal turned back to her. "No, I told you at the beach. She slipped. It was an accident."

"It was *you!*" Meg nearly started laughing, at the sheer audacity of that thought. Crazy was a word she had heard tossed around her whole life, but now she resolved never to use it again. Crazy wasn't laughing too loudly or playing a game with too much intensity. Crazy was this: this man, who saw the world differently than everyone else. Who was dangerous, and not only got away with it, it didn't even keep him up at night. He was *delusional.* "I know it was you, you pushed her!"

Cal just shook his head. Even with the movement, his eyes remained focused on her, narrowed, blind to everything else. Churning and endless as the sea. It swept her up, dragged her under, that focus. "She fell," he said, mostly to himself. Meg had expected a lot of things, a lot of reactions, but not this. Not real, defiant denial.

He took a step closer to her; that thing rose in her chest, fiercely, clawing at her throat to escape. *Back. Back. Back.* She couldn't. She couldn't move.

"But you came," he said, and his gaze dropped so abruptly she shuddered. But it fell not to her body, but to her feet. To the white sandals, and when he looked back up there was something reverent in his eyes. "And you... you spoke like her. You looked at me like... like she did. And I knew."

Another step. Meg swallowed but her mouth was dry enough it took two tries. "Knew what?" she asked, raising her head so he had to look her in the eye. It stopped him for a second. Maybe the videos were wrong, if she looked at him the same way as his fiancée, because the emotions were opposite. She couldn't love him. Maybe Eliza didn't either. Maybe that was why she was dead.

His laugh stuttered out and died, but the hope on his face didn't. "You're my second chance."

Her heart dropped down into her stomach with dread.

He'll kill you last.

"I... don't understand," she stalled, looking at Mr. Arud instead—but the coward dropped his gaze and turned mostly around, like if he didn't see it, it wasn't happening. "Cal, I'm not Eliza!"

"But you're so much like her." There was so much *hope* in his eyes, when he said that, when he stared at her. It didn't make any sense. He had *killed her.* Why would he want her back if he had done that? Was his regret really that strong? That was what everything else seemed to point to. Maybe.

But... she could deal with a crazy person better than a sane one. Crazy people just had to hear what they wanted to hear. As long as she didn't interrupt the illusion, she was safe inside it.

It tore at her, but she managed a smile. "Maybe... Maybe I could be," she managed. "But... then why am I tied up?"

"Precaution." And he finally was too ashamed to look her in the eye anymore, looking down at his hands the way he had on the beach. Like he was noticing them for the first time, had never paid them much mind before. "I... I didn't kill them. I swear I didn't. They were accidents."

"How could you *not?*" She reined her temper back in and tried again. Poise. This was balanced on the edge of a knife. If it fell, she died. "I was *there.* You were standing *right next* to Jay! How was that not you?"

"I don't know. All I can tell you is... it was going to happen either way. If it wasn't me, it was going to be an accident." He looked back up at her, his gaze deep and fathomless. "Things happen for a reason."

There was a disconnect between the terrible words and the flat calmness of his face, something past good acting. It was a sensation that she actually remembered, herself, from watching the videos. The way she was in the story, and then the unthinkable happened and she wrenched herself free in an instant. *This can't be real. This can't be happening to me.* She could hear those same words in his silence now. Denial was a powerful thing.

It was also an excuse.

"You're the reason," Meg said, "The reason for all of them! For all of this! How do you not *see it?*"

"She's not going to understand." Mr. Arud spoke for the first time. His voice was low, measured, impossibly calm. Suddenly she was sure: he was complicit in all of it, even Eliza. No one should handle this so well. He didn't even look surprised. "We should move on."

"Where is Beth?" Meg repeated, willing her voice not to shake. They were talking about killing her. She wanted to at least have something to keep her strong until they did. "Can you please tell me that, Cal? Is she safe?"

Instead of answering, he just stared at her, like she was missing something crucial. Mr. Arud looked up at the ceiling and shifted further back into his corner.

"This house is very old," Cal said, never looking away from her eyes. "There are more tunnels beneath the floor just like the ones you went through. And when it rains, they fill with water."

What did that have to do with Beth?

And then she heard it again in the pause: the low, rhythmic scratching.

It sent icy shudders all over her skin. That sound was wrong. Everything about it was. She thought it was a rat, but not when it was that measured, over and over again. *Scratch. Scratch. Scratch.* It reminded her of when she and Beth had taken her cat to the vet, and, trapped in the box, desperate, it had scraped against the plastic sides over and over again, short scuffs, nails grating against her nerves...

But it wasn't something scratching. It was some*one.*

Beth.

No. No, no, no, no, no, please—

"She's..." *Dying,* she wanted to say, but everything was too quiet, it was moving too fast. She couldn't breathe, she couldn't speak, she couldn't move. Beth. Beth. Beth. She had to do something. She had to save her.

Cal blinked back at her, impassive, uncaring, without looking down at his feet. Now that she knew what he was standing on, she could see the glimmer of water beneath his feet. There was no air down in the tunnels he was talking about.

Beth was just an inconvenience, another person to cross off his list so he could do what he wanted.

The fingernails clawed again. Sharper. Like a pane of glass breaking in half. Like a heart attack. It was loud, desperate, the sound of everything falling apart.

"Please," she whispered, focusing on the sound because it meant she was alive, it meant there was a chance. *I'll do anything. Just don't kill her.* Why wouldn't her damn tongue work?

Because there was no way to save her—because Cal didn't care about her. She had known all along. So had Beth. That was why they had run. That was why she had a knife.

Cal said, slowly, as though she was a child not understanding him, "I don't need her."

Murderer.

"Please!"

"I don't need her."

I do.

It felt like a star exploding in her chest, up her throat, roaring in her ears, filling every inch of her—growing in intensity, ripping into her soul, until all she knew was a burning, rooted rage deep inside of her. But the rage was tainted, brittle, with a kind of horror she had only dreamed about. There was time but she couldn't move, he wouldn't listen...

Cal's face was expressionless, emotionless, not even looking down at the floorboards.

"Please..."

And then there was nothing.

But silence.

Chapter Twenty-Three

When there was no sound from the floorboards, no scratching, no desperate gasp for air, no movement at all, it was like everything inside of Meg shifted into alignment. Alignment with what she wanted, what she *really* wanted. Not survival at any cost, the way she thought she did as the others in her group were picked off. Then, with everything feeling so fragile, she had clung to her own breath, her own heartbeat, her own thoughts and actions as the concrete reminders that she was still here. She didn't want to let go of anything, but she would. She just wanted out, like a trapped animal.

When the sound stopped, things snapped into clarity. She didn't want survival. She wanted more.

"Y-you killed her."

"She wasn't—"

"You *killed her!*"

Cal stopped. Meg clenched her fists tight enough her knuckles burned, and her vision blurred with more than tears. Was this the purpose Beth had felt, when she said they needed to split up and knew exactly what it meant? It was powerful.

She was going to feel it for the rest of her life.

"I don't care what you say lives inside you," Meg said, the rage raising her voice, "You're still human. You can still die. You can still be killed. And I'm going to be the one to do it."

Cal started to smile.

"You shouldn't throw words like that around," he said. "They have weight."

"Then understand that I fucking *mean them.*"

His eyes narrowed, more playful than menacing still. "Dangerous words."

"*I mean them.*"

Mr. Arud shifted behind them, but didn't say anything. Meg stared Cal down, aware of him and the dark around him like they were the same entity. It should have felt menacing, maybe; she should have been more cautious, probably. She couldn't. She didn't want to. The stakes didn't matter anymore.

Finally, Cal sighed. "You'll change your mind."

If there was a single thing he could say that scared her more than "I'm going to kill you now," it was that. It was the housekeeper's words coming true. *He'll kill you last.*

"I don't understand," she managed after a long second. "Aren't you going to... to..." She couldn't make herself say it. Not when it was so immediate, a very real possibility.

Cal, though, looked at her, sizing her up, making decisions, and said, "No. You're going to stay with us."

No. No, no, no, absolutely not, she was not going to be his *prize.* Beth didn't die so this man could win and keep her or kill her at his whim.

"No," she said, gritting her teeth. "No. I'd rather die."

Cal smiled—the same smile he'd been giving her all weekend, his normal one, but it felt different with the shadows dripping into his face like tar filling a mold. Nothing sinister about it except the circumstances. "It's not really your choice."

In the corner of the room, Mr. Arud stepped forward and then back again as he changed his mind. There was something he wanted to say—that he didn't agree. He didn't want her to live. But he was... scared of Cal? Afraid of stepping close to something too raw and triggering more violence?

Meg took a deep breath, steadying herself against the chair. *You know them,* she thought to calm her shaking nerves. *Knowledge is power. Use it.*

"Mr. Arud," she said, watching him jump, "What do you think? Am I a good enough new daughter-in-law? Or prisoner?"

His face, for someone who was holding her hostage, looked oddly guilty at last. "I..."

Cal frowned, halfway glancing over his shoulder. "Dad?"

"We can't do this," he said under his breath, fast, taking a quick step back as if he wanted to sprint. "I'm sorry, Cal, but I'm putting my foot down on this. She's not staying with us."

Cal turned to his father with deliberate slowness. There was no anger in his face, but Meg felt it in the lack of anything at all.

"She's my second chance," he said. "I'm not losing her this time."

*You didn't **lose** her last time,* Meg thought fiercely, but she didn't say anything. Eyes straight forward so Mr. Arud wouldn't say anything, she twisted her hands behind her back.

Not aimlessly, anymore. Not uselessly. Down.

Mr. Arud lifted his head and steeled himself. "Think logically, Cal. She'll talk. It has to be all of them, so we can explain it the right way."

"She can't talk if she's with us."

A fresh spike of fear. Meg forced her hands again, down and forward—toward the tiny pocket in the back of the dress, and her knife. She was able to grasp the handle and flip it open, but it took some concentration to start sawing at the rope tying her hands together. She could cut herself loose—assuming they were distracted that long, and she wasn't shaking so hard she dropped it.

"And if she gets out, we're ruined. We have to kill her."

"*I. Said. No.*"

Who did she want to win, she wondered. There was no winning. Unless she could... cut this...

Mr. Arud shrank a little under his son's stare, but with a quick glance at Meg (she stopped sawing and froze) he straightened again. "I've given you a lot, Cal," he said, calm, each word calculated and deliberate, like placing a chess piece. He had been doing this for long enough he knew the right way: walking around his son like he was walking on glass, waiting, dreading for it to happen again, maybe to him this time. "I've done a lot for you. This is all I want in return. For you not to give it all up for a *delusion.*"

Cal's eyes narrowed dangerously.

She could move her hands a bit more freely. So close. So close but every second Cal and his father stared each other down stretched on for eons. They were deciding her fate and by the time they chose she needed to be free and ready to run.

"I'm not giving her up this time," Cal said. "I *won't.*"

Such certainty, in his tone. It sent shivers crawling down her spine, like spiders under her skin—but she could use it. She could buy a little more time.

"Mr. Arud," she said, taking a chance, "I promise you, if you don't kill me now, I'll *ruin you.* Ruin you, and Cal, and your entire family name, and everything associated with it. I'll get out and everyone will find out what you both did here tonight!"

He narrowed his eyes at her, but it wasn't menacing. It was calculating, a seasoned businessman deciding which strategy to take. He looked back up at Cal and shook his head. "You have to think about this, Cal. Please. Logically. How much is she really worth to you?"

Meg didn't dare wait for the answer. She yanked her hand down so far her wrist felt broken and sliced through the rope and her skin at the same time. She didn't care. She barely felt it.

Mr. Arud said something lost in her movement, and Cal spun around to look at her.

Meg turned and bolted up the stairs and slammed the door shut behind her.

Chapter Twenty-Four

Don't open. Don't open. Don't open.

She could have run, but she didn't know where to go, what to do, so she grabbed the first thing she saw—a mop—and jammed it under the handle. Through the adrenaline, the rage, her blood pounding hot through her veins so fast she was shaking, it stuck. The handle wasn't moving. Not even if they rammed the door. Not before she could run.

She couldn't make herself run, though. Not yet.

The door handle twitched sideways, once, twice, and then stopped.

"There's nowhere for you to go," Cal said, voice low and satisfied, "You know that, right?"

Meg breathed out, shuddering, clutching her stomach to hold herself upright. *You can't fall yet. Not yet.*

Beth.

"Why?" she choked.

No answer. This was all a part of his game. A part of who he was. What he did couldn't be justified, even if he did answer her.

It was for nothing. It always was.

Her focus changed. Sharpened. Cut into her like a knife and the pain woke her straight up, a crack of lightning in the dark.

"You're not going to kill me," she said out loud.

Cal laughed once; she felt it through the door, and every muscle in her body locked up. "That's not your choice," he said, and his voice slid through the darkness. Made it living and dangerous. "It's *my* house. *I* know it. And I can make anything happen."

Meg swallowed, hard, and turned to face the door. "You killed Beth," she spat. "And the last thing she told me to do was to make you pay. And I intend to."

He laughed again, sounding almost caught off guard. Like just because she wore a dress and smiled at him, she shouldn't have had any bite. People fought for their lives. She would do the same.

"You should let me leave," Meg said, voice louder, stronger, "Because I'm going to fight you, every step of the way. And I'm going to win."

This time, for the first time, Cal was silent. Considering. She didn't dare hope he was going to listen but the recognition made her stand up straighter, clench her fists tighter.

"Fine," he said. "Then try to win."

She heard his footsteps moving away, to find a new way out to get to her, and she opened up a panel in the wall and slipped inside.

Meg didn't dare stop until she was a floor up—although she wouldn't have known that if she hadn't taken the stairs. There were three levels, and each level looked the same, a damn labyrinth, nearly impossible to navigate in the dark. And none of the stairs were next to each other. There were more, there was a way further up, but she couldn't remember them. Her brain felt... scrambled. Scattered. Going in five different directions and if she didn't just keep running, one hallway after another, she was going to stop and not start again.

And then she would die. And that just wasn't an option.

Meg kept running, until she reached a room that might have been a dining room in a former life. There was a huge dining table in the center, dark oak with sweeping legs that curled up under the flat top, and without hesitation she used her waning adrenaline and shoved it over. It fell against the door with a resounding crash that rattled the house and knocked dust off of the ceiling and sent the sheets sweeping against the floor. It would tell Cal and his father where she was but she didn't have it in her to care. They couldn't move that. They would have to find a back way in.

She had to stop. Had to. She couldn't get her breath back and everything was going blurry.

Shivering, Meg looked around the room. The walls were moving in and out, closer and further from her in throbbing strokes, and she gasped down dusty, cold air and leaned against one of the end tables. There were things on it, glasses and plates and silverware, stored as if somebody might walk in and set them out one day on a whim, and one of the glasses started to roll sideways toward the ground. She grabbed for it on instinct—Why? Why even bother? He knew she was here. Even if he hadn't heard the table crash over the thunder and roar of the wind, he would find her. He knew the house. He knew everything in it. He knew where she was, what she was going to do, that she was an animal with its leg caught in a snare...

Breathe. He's just a person.

She didn't know that. He wasn't just a person, he was a crazy person, a desperate person who knew he was going to jail for the rest of his life if Meg escaped, and that made him even more dangerous. She should have guessed. She should have known.

The room was fluctuating again. The walls were grainy and not just with the dust in the air.

Breathe, she ordered herself, holding the glass tight to her chest, every muscle in her body wanting to snap and collapse her to the ground so she would never move again, *breathe.*

A fever dream. That was what this was. Any second now she was going to wake up. She just had to shake her head just right, cause herself a little pain to snap out of it, scream a little louder until the ringing in her ears drowned out her heart...

No. No, her fingers curled into her palms dug in like spikes. Her breathing was loud, echoed in the tiny room. Her head was moving like it should have, the scenery around her wasn't changing, she was still trembling but everything moved right. Nothing was off the way it felt in a dream—except everything. Everything was wrong. Everything was too immediate and too sharp and that meant... it was real.

It was really happening.

What she had heard...

Beth.

Meg whirled around and hurled the glass at a mirror and screamed, tearing the sorrow out of her chest and up her throat, so loud that when the glass shattered it was soundless. The mirror didn't fall at once, like she expected, like she wanted, but splintered and cracked branching out in spider webs. Where the glass hit, the shards had fallen away to reveal the stark wooden base so that there was a hole in the side of her face.

That was what it felt like. Like she had been split down the middle, like a piece of her she had always taken for granted had been torn away. The cracks ran across and splintered her face into all different directions, and the small bit she could see was tear-streaked and dirty. Like someone had dug her out of the ground.

Beth.

Her mind roiled, full of rage and sorrow and fear, but all she could think of was that silence. Echoing around her like she was in the bottom of a well. She had run away without seeing... her, and in equal parts she was grateful and sure she was a coward for being grateful. The right thing to do was take responsibility for it. For all of it.

She was only here because of me. She's only dead because I didn't understand what someone with nothing to lose can do.

Now she understood. Now she knew, too late—and so would everyone. So would the house and all the dead and secrets buried up inside it. So would Cal.

She watched, like it was happening to someone else, her own face contort through the cracks in the mirror, warped to such an extent that her own mind tolled out a warning. *Something is wrong.*

Yes, she thought, *I am what's wrong.*

I'm not going to die here.

CHAPTER TWENTY-FIVE

Meg pushed herself into a corner, held her knife like a child held a security blanket, and thought. She pushed her mind to focus—clearer, sharper, every test she had ever aced but with higher stakes. Focus. What was it she needed to do? Where could she even the odds? They had the house, they had the keys, they had the numbers...

Numbers first. That was the thing that had her jumping out of her skin at every creak and every movement. She had forgotten that Mr. Arud would be on the side of his son even if he was insane, that he was the same type of desperate. She couldn't run until daybreak if they could divide and conquer, especially now that it was just her.

But she had to move.

Legs. She had to get her legs to move forward, out of her safe corner—it wouldn't be safe for long anyways, she knew that, it was just hard not to stay there anyways—and toward the door...

She didn't move.

She was going to kill them. She knew that, in a dark part of her mind, with a voice growing louder and colder. She had to kill one of them so they couldn't ambush her. She had to kill them because they had killed Beth. Mourning could come later, when she was safe. Now it was rage fueling her and she had plenty of kindling.

No one would recognize her when she came back. But she wasn't afraid. People became what they needed to in order to survive—to win. She had to.

Meg shivered, trying not to look around the room too hard. She recognized it—she was close to where she had started. Right outside, one hallway over, would be where… where Jay's body was. She was going to have to pass it.

She was going to find what had happened to Kendra, she realized with a jolt. Kendra, the police officer that, to her knowledge, Cal still didn't know had been here. Maybe she had something she could use in her pocket that Cal wouldn't have thought to look for. Another knife. A gun. A phone that had better service than a regular cell phone so she could call for help.

It was worth a look. But in order to do that, she had to move.

She had to talk to herself like she was a child. Simply. No-nonsense. *You stop when I tell you to stop.* She didn't want to move but she had to.

Meg closed her eyes.

You're going to get up, she bargained with herself, *on the count of three. One, two…*

On three (maybe four, maybe five, she stopped counting), she pushed herself up. Her legs felt sturdy, not broken like she had expected; it was all in her head. It was all in how she breathed, how she told herself to move or not to move and what to do.

She had lived her whole life in her head. She knew how to direct it: the same way you did everything else. One step at a time.

Walk. You want to live. You're going to do this.

Slowly, she moved toward the door.

She didn't see Kendra's body at first. She saw Jay's.

There was a tiny part of her, the part that felt young and knew exactly how over her head she was, that had been hopeful that he wasn't actually dead. It had fallen on him, yes, his neck had turned too much, but she hadn't seen any blood. She hadn't stayed long enough to see if he was breathing. She had hoped, in the back of her head as she started running, *he's just in shock and he'll wake up and be okay.*

When she reached the great room and saw the clock, and the form underneath it in the same awkward collage of angles on the floor, Meg let that scrap of hope go. Cal had killed him just like he had intended to.

I'm sorry, Meg thought, but she forced herself to move on. There was no time to feel sorrow or show him any respect unless she intended to join him. Now there was only finding Kendra. She had lunged at Cal, and though it sounded like she had fought him for several minutes while she and Beth had run, she couldn't have gone far. Maybe out the hallway... No, not there, but there were stairs here...

She was on the stairs just outside, skewered through the chest.

Meg gasped and recoiled backwards. She had expected something... smaller, somehow. More subtle, like the others had been. Not Kendra. Kendra had been run through with a piece of the railing on one of the staircases, sharpened like a stake, and it was as thick around as a pole. She had fallen onto it—or more likely been pushed by Cal—but the diameter of it, and the force with which it had to have been run through her, looked unnatural. It felt like much more of an event.

The others had been done by a person, suddenly enough they could be (or had been, in Bill's case) an accident, one quick snap and then done. This could have been done by something more than human—or less than.

Meg swallowed nausea—there was so much blood, dark and viscous, soaked through Kendra's t-shirt and a shallow, still pool at her feet—and inched forward. She was here with a purpose. She had something she needed to look for. She needed to go through Kendra's pockets... She just had to pretend she was alive, not think about it, not touch the skin and feel how cold it was or if it was still warm...

The pocket was damp. She gagged and patted it down, quick, and found a cell phone in her front left pocket.

She pulled it out and turned it on. It was on low battery, but there was no service. She had hoped for otherwise, that maybe she had been lying and saying she had no service so she didn't stand out. She took it anyways for the light.

Meg swallowed and looked in her coat pockets next, trying not to linger too long on the expression on her face just above, slightly shocked and sad with her eyes still staring open at the ceiling. There was nothing in the right pocket, but in the left pocket there were a couple scraps of paper.

Carefully, Meg pulled them out. They were soaked through on the edges with blood, but it was clear they were both photos, and the pictures were still visible.

The first was of Eliza, taken with an older camera and printed as an instant Polaroid, and she was standing in her white dress and sandals with a giant floppy sunhat. She was grinning at the camera and the person holding it (Cal, it had to be, that was who it always was) and standing on the edge of the beach cliff that Cal was later going to push her off of.

Meg turned it over.

Barely visible on the reverse side, soaked through with blood, was someone's caption for the picture. It was in the same looping handwriting as the memory box Meg had found downstairs, which meant it was written by Eliza herself.

Me in my new home! I can't wait to spend forever here!

She didn't know where Kendra had found this, if it had been in the house or was a piece of evidence, but it was clearly her handwriting. She didn't know who Cal was, had no inclination she was going to die. She was just a girl blindly in love.

The second was a family photo, one that Meg recognized from the memory box she had found in the basement. It was clearly a different copy, though, because there was a message on the back, too. Names of the people in the picture.

One of the names was *Aunt Kendra.*

Meg bit her lip against any tears that tried to escape. It explained so much about Kendra and Jay, why they hadn't left in spite of the danger and the high stakes when any normal person would have. Now that Beth was gone, she understood. Rage was a powerful, blinding force.

Grief even more so.

Meg tucked them in her pocket carefully. Eliza was only one of the people that Cal needed to answer for now, but she was going to make sure this survived. Kendra and Jay had died for it. It was the least she could do.

They wouldn't need any more proof after tonight, though; everyone was going to know what Cal was. There was only whether Meg was alive to tell them herself.

It took every ounce of willpower she possessed, but she somehow managed to reach out and close Kendra's eyes. She was dead, there was no way she wasn't, but it looked like she was going to wake up any second still. Her arms were open, like she had been reaching forward when she died. Even with no chance of living, it was her instinct to try to get help. To reach out to someone in her last moment of life.

Beth had tried, too.

Meg bit her lip, hard, to ground herself in the present. Beth was dead because she had given Meg her chance. She wouldn't throw it away now.

She had to get out. She had to survive. *Make him pay.*

For the dead. She had to.

When she was in high school, Meg had to ride the city bus to work in the library. Their city wasn't big, but it had never felt so imposing as when she shrank into a seat, surrounded by adults who knew what they were doing and sat tall and powerful, their eyes raking over her critically and then back forward. She remembered sitting across from a man who had long white hair and watery gray eyes who smiled at her like a piece of meat so that she hugged her bag to her chest. She remembered a teenage boy sitting behind her and feeling like there was a gun to her head. She remembered holding keys in her hand like daggers.

This was the same feeling: small, backed into a corner, baring her teeth and aware if she lunged she would be killed. If her hands hadn't been frozen around the knife she would have dropped it.

She hated it. She couldn't afford to be small, not now, not with these kinds of things bearing down on her. Murderers, and ghosts, and panic, and sudden-fall fear that enveloped her entire brain. She had to be bigger. Braver. More ferocious than the things trying to kill her.

(Beth would be braver.)

Meg ran and ran, and felt, at the back of her mind, that it might be better for her to stand still and wait. It wasn't just that her footsteps were too loud in the suffocating silence made all the more acute by the driving forces outside; it was that on top of it the floorboards creaked, sharp and high like an animal in pain, and she heard the sounds echoing behind her. She rounded one corner and the hinges on the closest door squeaked too. The house wanted them to find her.

She tried to focus, she really did, but she had no idea where to go. She had a vague idea of where to avoid, from where she had been, but she didn't know where Cal and Mr. Arud were. She might run into them, and if she did, she didn't know how it would go. Likely badly. She had a pocketknife and that wouldn't afford her much against two men, both bigger and stronger than her.

Her foot caught—ripped through the floorboard—and she hit the ground sprawling, hard enough it rattled her bones. She managed to only squeak under her breath instead of the profound swearing she wanted, soft enough to be lost under the sounds of the storm. Beneath her hands, though, the house was still ringing with her fall: a gunshot in a still forest, telling everyone where the danger was.

She scrambled to her feet, her blood pumping hot through her veins, and ran even faster. There was no thought for any direction at all anymore. Just *away*. They would hear that, and if they were close at all...

Mr. Arud emerged from her left, surprisingly fast for his age and injured leg, and that time Meg did scream. *No one left to hear—*

He grabbed for her wrists, and things woke up in her mind that she hadn't known were sleeping. How to fight dirty. How not to care about anything but him *letting go.*

Meg whipped her head all the way back until she hit his nose, felt it crack. He swore; his grip loosened and then tightened again, like manacles.

She buckled her knees, and he stumbled under the weight of his bad leg. When he was already off balance, she spun around and kicked out at it again, and that time he let go. Meg took off running as fast as she could—

But she had gotten turned around, and there was a wall.

Cal appeared from out of the shadows; her heart caught in her throat so suddenly she choked. "I'm impressed."

Meg swallowed and retreated a step when Mr. Arud moved to fill the rest of the hallway so there was nowhere for her to run. It was satisfying to see the blood drip down his face. Even more so to know she had done it.

But the *panic*, screaming at her...

"Don't come any closer," she said, but her voice was shaking so bad it barely came out. One of them was bad enough. Now that she was outnumbered... *"Don't."*

They weren't taking her seriously. Their faces didn't change at all. Cal took a step closer to her. So did his father.

Meg held her ground, somehow. They were wolves, moving in for the kill, and striking would do nothing, in the end. She was smaller, and weaker, and had no practice in violence. She had to be smarter than them, not stronger.

The closer they moved to her, though, the more she realized they weren't wolves at all. Wolves moved together, and Cal and his father, when they stepped closer to her, were moving different ways. Cal was closing the gap between her and them, and Mr. Arud was moving toward her but trying to stay away from his son.

He was afraid of him.

She had to get them talking. That had divided them so she could escape before. She had to do the same thing again. Beth had always been good at this. If she was here...

But she's not.

Meg straightened. Control. Power. "Are you going to kill me like you killed Eliza?"

Cal stopped. "I didn't—"

"You did," Meg interrupted, and gestured to Mr. Arud, who stopped. Guiltily. "He knows it."

Cal whipped around to his father, who barely inclined his head in a shake. Like his body was frozen. He knew exactly what kind of animal his son was. There was a reason there were no knives in the kitchen, no tools in the basement, nothing that she could use as a weapon in the entire house. Those boxes in the basement were empty, she knew now, because he had bought them, used them, and then gotten rid of them. That was fear that she had never understood before today, and he felt it every day.

"She's lying," Mr. Arud said, and Cal looked back at her, waiting for what she was going to say. He wasn't *listening,* though. When it came down to it, she knew, he was going to believe his father, and then he was going to do whatever he wanted.

So she reached inside herself, pulling from that horrible part of her that knew him, that trusted him almost, because it was the part of her that drew him in turn. The serenity of when they had stood over the beach and walked the tide, the crushing need for her to be okay when he saved her life that was real and raw, how he truly believed she was his chance at redemption even as he killed her best friend. All of it. He wasn't the only one who could be something else if it would keep him alive, no matter how it tore at her soul.

For Beth. She was doing this for Beth.

"Cal. I'm telling you the truth."

"She's not," Mr. Arud interrupted, "Cal—"

"You know I am," Meg insisted. His eyes snapped sideways onto hers and it took everything she had to keep from flinching. If she loved him, if she was worth trusting, she wouldn't avoid his gaze. "Cal. I think you've always known, as soon as you saw Eliza…"

"No," Cal blurted. The look on his face was wretched enough she almost pitied him. The truth he had buried was clawing its way back up. "No. I wouldn't. I loved her."

"Exactly." Mr. Arud took a step toward his son. It was cautious; he knew, right now, that he was volatile. He was going to snap, one way or the other. Kill one of them. "Exactly. You loved her. And she fell and it was an *accident*. You *know that*."

Cal hesitated.

"He's lying," Meg said, meeting his eyes, making herself hold it and suppress her shudder. He was human, but now that she knew what he was capable of, he didn't look it. They felt both more than human and less. She didn't know how to quantify what killing did to someone's soul. "Cal. Look at me. He's lying to you and I'm telling you the honest to God truth. *Believe me.*"

"She's trying to confuse you—" When Cal spun around to turn his icy stare on his father he froze. Stopped and had to breathe deep to compose himself. He was slipping. "Cal. What happened to Eliza was an accident. You know that. *I* know that. You would never hurt her. You loved her."

Cal bit his lip and turned back to Meg, uncertainty twisting him human again. "I did love her."

"Maybe," Meg allowed, swallowing. He looked vindicated, satisfied, like loving her was something he had earned and absolved him of killing her, and that, that was what was wrong with him. He had loved Eliza, maybe, but as a beautiful thing to treasure, made all the more precious when he broke her and moved on. Moved on to Meg, who had appeared just so he could start the cycle over again. Love her until he killed her.

She wouldn't be another mystery for someone else to solve.

"It doesn't matter if you loved her," she said, holding her ground when every muscle itched to back up against the wall. She had a part to play. She looked Cal straight in his eyes, chilling in their focus and near glowing in the dark, and thought *I'm going to tell him nothing but the truth. He'll see that.*

I'll break him with it.

"You still killed her."

For the first time, he didn't immediately protest. Instead his face grew paler even in the low light, his anger diminishing.

Meg held her ground and felt her face slip into sympathy. It was easy, but she didn't let it stop her.

"You came up behind her," she said softly; his whole body shuddered, panic flashing over his face. And memory. "And she didn't even turn and look at you because she trusted you so much and she was just enjoying the view of the ocean..."

"Stop." Cal took a step back. Her gap was widening, bit by bit. But she had to keep pushing. He deserved to feel this, the brutal hit of the truth.

"And maybe at first you were just going to join her," Meg continued, taking a step toward him. She remembered the moments that it had felt so innocent, before it all went wrong. "But you didn't. She turned around and looked at you just to smile—"

"*No!*"

The whole house echoed with his shout this time, suddenly enough that Meg cringed backwards; dust fell from the ceiling and clouded in the air between them. He seemed like he was holding his breath, and the look on his face was so terrible that Meg knew, this time, he understood.

"You pushed her," Meg said. "It wasn't an accident, it was *you.*"

Cal's head swiveled toward his father, expression strained with desperation, and this time, when he needed him to tell him it was a lie, he didn't say anything. She could see it all on his face, the alibi, as clearly as if she was watching it herself.

Mr. Arud taking the camera from his son's hands as he came back to himself just like he had after he pushed the clock over and killed Jay. Saying the word 'accident' over and over again until Cal believed him. Getting rid of every trace of her to try to clean it up, to make sure he never remembered, to protect his son the only way he knew how.

Just a little farther and something was going to break.

"You knew, didn't you?" she asked Mr. Arud quietly.

His gaze snapped back onto hers, cold and guarded. "I don't know what you're talking about."

"Of course you do," Meg said, and the more she talked, the more she thought about the simple fact that he knew and kept it a secret from his son and things started to click in her head. "You knew the whole time. What else do you know about that he doesn't?"

That time, Mr. Arud took a step back away from his son so fast Meg was surprised he didn't stumble. Cal just stared at him, like he was seeing him for the first time.

"A lot of accidents happen in this house, like what happened to Kendra or me. But what about accidents like Eliza's?" She thought about what she had learned, from them and from her research and from the videos. The lore around this house... some of it wasn't the house. "What about ones that happened before her? Did the house talk to you before it talked to Cal?"

He laughed his businessman's laugh, like she was being ridiculous. Meg, though, had never been surer of anything. There was something here. There was nervousness in his voice. "You're reaching. I hid it to protect him."

"But you did know," Cal said, barely a whisper. "And... you lied to me?"

Meg kept the opening in her sights as their focus turned away from her. She had to wait for just the right moment to make a break for it. It was almost there.

And then it came to her. One of the stories she wasn't supposed to know.

"Cal," she asked quietly, "How did your mom die?"

She was afraid she had pushed too far, for a moment, as Cal's face went slack with shock.

Mr. Arud looked like he wanted to lunge at her, to silence her, but Cal was between them. Now, instead of caging her into the dead end, it was protecting her from him, so she could keep talking.

"It was..." Cal swallowed, hard. "An accident. Dad said..."

"But he lied to you before," Meg said, keeping her voice smooth even as her heart hammered in her chest. She knew things, now. Things that even they didn't. "She didn't like this house as much as you did, did she? And maybe it didn't like her. Just like Eliza."

"Stop," Mr. Arud blurted, backing up a step, "Stop, you don't know what you're doing..."

We came here for summers before my mom died. Only summers. She had been trying to take him away from it, just like Eliza.

"And just like Eliza," Meg said, contemplative and gentle, readying herself, "He pushed her."

And right when he needed it, Mr. Arud's voice failed him. His mouth opened and closed, but all that came out was a whisper.

"I'm... sorry."

Cal lunged for his father, face twisting into a snarl.

And Meg took the opening behind him and sprinted, faster than she ever had in her life, for the empty hallway behind them.

Nobody grabbed her. Nobody stopped her. Behind her, Mr. Arud was screaming, guttural and choking—*the way Beth must have died*—but Cal was silent. She kept going and the screaming grew fainter, the sounds of struggle fading into chilling stillness with no witnesses.

Chapter Twenty-Six

Meg didn't care where she went as long as it was away; she didn't know how long her distraction would last before they realized what she was doing and turned on her again. She couldn't hear them almost immediately turning the corner, and it was disorienting to suddenly feel alone when she knew, with something that was so sure it felt like precognition, that she wasn't. If they weren't following her yet, they would be soon. And what did she do when they did? Did she keep running? Hide? Fight?

No, fighting hadn't gone well. If she tried to take them head-on, she was going to lose every time; she had to think smarter than that. An ambush was the best thing she could think of—give them a taste of what it felt like to be hunted, their surroundings turning into a trap—but she wasn't sure her knife would give her any advantage. And she didn't know how to set it.

One of the floorboards creaked under her foot and she skittered sideways; this time it didn't break, and Meg breathed out and resisted the childish urge to swear at the floor. Everything in this damn house was determined to break underneath her...

Wait. There was her ambush.

A place appeared in her mind's eye and she backtracked to set her trap.

The thing that she saw that could most easily become lethal was something that she already knew could be dangerous: a chandelier, just like the one that had nearly taken out Kendra's eye with a glancing blow. There was one in another of the grand rooms, and she followed the map in her head until she was one floor above it. She hacked away at the floor with her knife until she uncovered the screw holding it up.

And then Meg poised to cut it free so that it would fall and crush them. Unlike the house, she wouldn't miss.

It would kill one of them. Hopefully Cal, because he had finished off his father. It had sounded final enough. But if he hadn't, she didn't care which. It would level the playing field. Give her a fighting chance.

It didn't matter.

She peered down through the hole she had made next to the chain, looking at Kendra's phone which she had set in the middle of the floor, and waited. Soon, it would bring him to the spot she needed him.

She was the hunter now.

After three minutes, Kendra's phone started to ring with an alarm. Meg waited, cringing at how the sound carried all through the house over the creaking and the storm outside. Cal would hear it. There was no way he wouldn't.

A few moments later, Cal came into her line of sight.

He moved through the room slowly, head swiveling from side to side, and Meg felt the last moment of indecision—not whether to spare him, but whether this would work. Did she chance it or...?

Yes.

I warned them.

Meg cut the cord.

Cal looked up, hearing the glass, but he didn't move. Meg wanted to close her eyes to it, but she couldn't.

She kept her eyes wide open as the steel frame crashed down—right next to him.

The pieces of glass rolled and skittered across the floor like cockroaches fleeing the light, into the corners of the room. It had tilted at the last moment—the house protecting him, just like he had known it would.

Everything was still.

"I didn't know you had it in you to kill," Cal said slowly. She had expected that there was nothing inside him, that was what she thought murderers had to be, but she knew when he stared at the attempt to kill him and was calm and composed. He wiped his face absently—wiped blood off. There wasn't a scratch on him.

Which made it his father's. And there was *nothing* in his eyes. Not a flicker.

Meg didn't reply. He didn't know she was here; he was just trying to get her to show herself. He only knew what she gave him, and she knew...

She knew everything. He had bared his soul to Eliza in the video, shown what it was he loved and what he was like underneath his mask, and Meg could see now that she had fallen in love with him, too, as she watched. He had been a mystery, an absent but integral part of the videos, and she had been intrigued by it. He had seemed so kind. So understanding. So all about Eliza, so obviously enamored with her, with such ferocity she had wished for her own love story with someone like him.

And then his last act was so violent, and all of the kindness was ripped out of him. Something had died in him, when he killed Eliza. It made him ugly. It made him terrible and inhuman.

"It gets easier," Cal said after a long moment.

Meg curled her hand into a tight fist to keep from rising to the bait. He was lying. It never got any easier to watch someone die, there was no way it got any easier to do it.

"Are you okay?" Cal asked, obscenely gentle. *Checking on her.*

"Do you have any idea how you sound?" she demanded. Her voice echoed in the cavernous room below her. "Do you even hear yourself?"

"I do." His face was sympathetic, his voice clear. "And it's really not as complicated as you think."

Meg laughed harshly. "The house talks to you. What's complicated about that?"

He sighed. "I was really hoping you'd understand."

He sounded almost sad, and it made Meg hesitate. It felt like holding a live grenade in her hand, dropping words down to him and hoping they had the right reaction.

But this was *not a game.*

"I understand plenty," she said. "I understand that you're dangerous and you need to be stopped."

A smile flickered over his face. "You think you're capable of that?"

Meg took a deep, bracing breath. The gamble was now.

"Yes," she said. "So come and get me. If you have the nerve."

Cal hesitated, considering. There was a smile on his face. The smile of someone who thought they had all the cards and couldn't lose.

He turned and started toward the staircase.

Meg turned and ran the other direction.

She had only minutes, and she knew where she was going with it.

Chapter Twenty-Seven

M eg was going back down to the basement.

It was a long shot, but it was all she could think of. If Jay's hunch had been right, the breaker would be in the basement, and since it wasn't in the one they had held her in then it would be in the one where she had found the box of Eliza's trinkets. And it was someplace she knew.

She ran back down the nearest staircase, but this time with purpose. If she could get down there, maybe she could get the power on so she could see. Maybe there was another way out. Maybe she could stay down there until things blew over. Maybe...

It didn't matter what maybe was down there anymore. She was just hoping for something, anything that could help her.

She reached the stairs back down to the basement and shut the door behind her as quietly as possible. Then locked it. Then stacked five boxes.

Then she took a step back and breathed out for the first time.

Okay. First, find the breaker.

She had no phone anymore, so she dragged her hand along the right wall, working her way down the stairs while feeling along it for anything. She squeezed behind the sheet-covered tables, chairs, mirrors, boxes, pieces of furniture people didn't even use anymore, and though she went all the way around the perimeter, there was nothing on the wall.

No breaker. Maybe the house had never even had one in the first place and Cal had just mentioned it to separate their group.

Meg sighed and rubbed the dust off her fingers on her dress. Next course of action, next plan...

Something fell off one of the tables behind her.

Meg whirled around, grabbing for her knife, but stopped before she could scream. Not Cal—it was too small for that. It was only the crow from the first time they were down here.

She breathed out heavily. "Shoo," Meg whispered, flapping her hand at it. "Shoo!"

Nothing. It was as still as a painting, its beady black eyes fixed on her alone. Now that she knew what it was, though, she was grateful it hadn't taken off. Cal would be listening for any noise—for her.

The crow tilted its head, looking at her with the same glassy-eyed stare as the dead upstairs; Meg hissed at it through her teeth, nearly silently, just enough to move its gaze. Birds of bad omen indeed. She should have grabbed Beth and run the second they found a bird like a wraith in his basement.

Meg forced her gaze up, away, and listened. The house creaked above her head, once, sharply... but that was just because it was old, she told herself, otherwise she couldn't breathe with the force of the sheer terror that washed over her. Cal hadn't found her yet. She would hear him. It actually burned at her, how he walked instead of ran after her, how he didn't mask his footsteps but let them echo so she was aware of them.

Meg started to pace, hoping it would jolt her brain into another idea. She had come down here because it was someplace he wouldn't expect. He didn't think he could be killed in his house, for whatever reason. (Don't think about it. She had no answers and no time to find them and they didn't matter.) He would keep looking until he found her.

Was there a trap she could set up down here? Something to at least slow him down, stall him, while she thought of something more permanent? No, the furniture was all too heavy for her to move, even if it didn't feel like disturbing a tomb. There was no vantage point for her to use this time. She had a knife but the idea of parting with it made her shake. She had nothing else.

There was a sharp but quiet tap behind her, and she spun around—but it was just the crow, moved down to the floor, picking at one of the wooden floorboards with its black beak. At her movement it stopped and considered her, one bright beady eye at a time, and then resumed. Like it had a purpose.

What was special about that one floorboard?

The crow pecked at the floorboard again, at the edge, and Meg walked cautiously toward it. Just like the ones at home, daring enough to grab food off the street and barely jump out of the path of her tires, it hopped just far enough away that she couldn't touch it but didn't fly away. Just kept looking at her.

Carefully, she leaned down to where it was pecking as it watched her from the edge of the shadows. It was impossible to see anything, but when she traced with her fingers she could just make out a few raised ridges on the floor. And just on the edges, it was colder. Like there was air coming up from *underneath*, and the crow could somehow feel it.

It was connected to the outside.

Meg laughed breathlessly and pried her fingers underneath the edge of the board; it creaked but didn't give, and fear gave her the strength to pull harder, the joints in her bones straining. She could do this. So close, so close, so close...

The boards came up all at once, and there was hollow space underneath it.

Filled with black, bottomless water.

Meg shuddered and jolted backwards, breathing hard to keep herself from screaming. Behind her, distant, the doorknob clicked but didn't turn.

This was how Beth had died. And now—now it was her only way out.

"I can't do it," Meg breathed. She didn't know who she was talking to—the crow?—but instead of grounding her, outside her racing mind, it echoed around the basement. She felt herself shrinking. "I can't do it. I can't..."

You have to.

She didn't know whose voice it was, but it was her own words. She didn't even know when she'd started to think like that. When they started to sound like daggers in her own head.

"I can't," she repeated, just to break the silence, just to feel safe for the first time in days. "I *can't.*"

You have to. Or you're going to die.

"I can't..."

You have to be brave.

She didn't want to be brave. She wanted to wake up.

You have to.

She had to. She had to. Beth had told her to live and if she was going to live she was going to have to get out.

He tried the door again. It felt closer. Louder. He was getting in.

It was his house. It wasn't going to hurt him. She was going to have to get out of the house.

She took a deep breath, grabbing the crow to her chest. It squawked and bit her fingers, sharp as thorns, and she held in a cry but didn't make a sound. She had to. If the crow had led her to this tunnel, it could lead him. She had to take it with her, even when she tried to hold its beak shut and its next bite made her finger bleed.

Please, she thought, putting in one foot; the water was so cold it froze her blood in her veins, and her toes went numb immediately, so much she wasn't sure she could run. Hypothermia. She was going to freeze to death and die. *Please. Please. Please. I don't want to die.*

The crow had stopped, maybe recognizing that she was going in its tunnel, going to take it outside. They were always said to be smart.

The door handle clicked again, louder, like a ticking time bomb.

Meg took a deep breath and lowered herself in.

Chapter Twenty-Eight

When Meg surfaced it took all of her willpower not to scream from the sheer *cold* of it. It was like someone was hammering pins and needles into every pore in her body at once, pricking into her nerves, driving her brain into nonstop *get out get out get out.* This was cold enough, if she didn't get out soon, it would kill her.

Like Beth. Don't think about it, don't think about it, don't think about it. If she added panic to this, she wasn't going to even be able to swim.

It took her a second to realize the crow was squawking in protest at being dunked, and she shivered and held its beak shut with one hand and reached up to the floor with the other. Her hands were numb already, her fingers were clumsy, but she somehow managed to pull the floorboard back into place. It left her in pitch total darkness.

She felt, if she stood on tiptoe, that the tunnel sloped slightly downward. It was up to the edge of her nose here, but it would probably get closer to the floorboards further down so that she wouldn't be able to breathe at all.

Meg shivered and thought *please God, if there is any mercy in the world, don't let me find Beth's body.*

Cal was in the basement. She could hear him, his footsteps creaking the floorboards above her head. Back and forth. Back and forth. Maybe he would assume she was gone.

The crow struggled against her hands, biting so deep at the sides of her fingers that it was pinching all the way down to the bone. Meg held its wings down, held its beak shut, but it was squirming out. It was squirming out and this water sapped her strength, she could feel it.

If it let Cal know she was here, she was going to die.

She held it under the water, far enough down that if it got out it wouldn't splash the water and give her away; the struggles increased, frenzied, and Meg choked down silent sobs. She couldn't do this. She knew what it was like to suffocate. She had heard Beth's panic as she drowned.

She twisted her hands in opposite directions. The first time it did nothing, her fingers slipping, and the beak snapped hard enough she thought for sure it was going to take her fingers off. The second time, she heard the muffled crack through the water.

She let it go, heard instead of saw it bob to the surface of the water and pushed the wet feathers away before they brushed against her face, feeling somehow both empty and full, pressing her lips tight together. All the screaming was inside her head, beating against the walls, unheard, unseen, unheeded. She couldn't panic now. She would die.

The floorboard above her creaked—he was here—and before she could talk herself out of it, Meg took a deep breath and dove under the water.

When it closed over her head, it was worse than anything she had felt in her life. She had never been this cold before, never been so sure that it was going to swallow her up like dirt on a grave, but she pushed her feet off the bottom and kicked. She could move faster swimming than walking. Maybe she could get a good enough head start toward the other end of the tunnel that Cal couldn't follow her before she had to surface—

No, wait, she had to surface in case the water was too high to breathe.

Meg pushed off the bottom, swimming up, and broke the surface at the same time her forehead hit the ceiling so that she coughed on water. She was already here—

Cal grabbed her hair behind her and pulled her under mid-breath.

She gasped, inhaling water so cold it was nearly ice when it went into her lungs. She couldn't breathe even if she wanted to, her lungs wouldn't function at all. Cal's hands dug deeper into her hair, pulling her down and holding her down, and she hadn't understood how much stronger he was than her until right now. Right now, when it mattered.

She was drowning. Drowning like Beth.

Panic gave her energy; she struck out with her elbows, with her fists, with her knees. None of them connected with anything lasting or solid (she couldn't find his eyes, couldn't see anything, she couldn't *breathe)* but the thrashing got her head above the water. She gasped one more breath—it tasted of mildew, and salt—before he pulled her back under.

If he's pulling me under to kill me, she realized suddenly, *then he doesn't have a weapon.*

She did.

She grabbed for his arm, felt where it was, and found his shirt in her hands. She held it so she didn't lose her bearings, and thrust her knife into his side as hard as she could.

She felt it connect, just barely; he let go with a short yell muffled by the water. She pushed off of him with both feet so that he went backwards and she propelled herself forwards.

Almost there. She had to be almost there, she was running out of air...

Meg broke the surface again, urgent, lack of breath filling her limbs with concrete, and this time it lifted so that she could taste air.

The way out.

She wasn't sure where she found the strength, but she pulled herself out by her elbows onto cold metal, the water weighing her dress down so heavily it almost tore off of her, slammed it shut on Cal's fingers—she heard him gasp for air before it closed, she had no idea such a simple sound could fill her with so much fury and so little pity—and stood on it. It was all she had, unless she could find something... A loop, made for a lock, was on the side of the door, and she tore a gardening stake free of the muddy ground and sealed it shut. Cal wouldn't be strong enough on his own to move it from the inside. He would have to go around.

She had a few minutes again. Instead of relief, though, what she wanted to do was scream. Was it too much to ask for Cal to just *drown?*

But he wouldn't. She could already tell. She shielded her eyes from the rain and wind and looked out behind her.

The fence was barely visible at the edge of the field: iron, seven feet tall, gated with a key that she didn't have and too high for her to climb. She could feel from the ground beneath her feet that it would be too tough for her to dig through before Cal found her. She had nothing to break it with.

She was outside, but she was still trapped.

This was it, Meg realized, and it dragged at her very bones and brought her to her knees in the mud. She didn't even have the energy left to sob. It had all been taken out of her, leeched out by the icy waters she felt dripping out of her mouth, ripped out like the gouges in her hands where the crow had clawed at her. She could still hear its neck snap, in the back of her mind, ringing with the horrible silence when Beth had gone. So much violence.

I tried, she thought, like a prayer. *Beth, I'm so sorry, I tried to save you. I should never have brought you along. It should have been me.*

She wanted it all to stop. She wanted to be home. She wanted to never have watched those tapes.

Almost in answer, though, an echo she couldn't keep from coming, that voice again. Herself, but stronger, more. *Keep moving. Keep going. You're so close.*

I don't want to be close. I want to be done.

But that voice kept urging her, kept prodding gently and awakening her instinct to survive one tiny jolt at a time, so she crawled forward. She crawled through a tunnel in the rose bushes, flattened to the ground by the storm, and their tiny thorns tore into her palms and knees and calves and stomach, like fire ants, finding every patch of bare skin.

She kept her eyes closed so she didn't blind herself, and kept crawling. It felt like nothing at all compared to the cold seeping through her skin to her organs, bone-deep. She could feel her energy waning, failing her.

Survival. That was what kept her crawling, one inch at a time, as webs tangled in her hair and it felt like Cal's footsteps rang on all sides of her. Not vengeance, a nice dream when she thought she was better than she was, survival. If only one of them was going to make it out of here alive, it was going to be her.

Just a little further.

By the time she reached the clearing past the tunnel, Meg's whole body was numb; her hands were scraped raw, her fingers bloody and trembling and nearly numb. Between the running, the crow, the roses, and the rain, she was surprised they still worked.

But she was alive. And if she was going to stay that way, she needed to keep going.

In the distance, barely visible between the rain and the dark, was a gazebo, open to the wind but sheltered from at least some of the rain. Maybe it was too predictable, it wasn't exactly easily defensible, but she had a few minutes before Cal followed her and found her, and she needed to breathe. She needed to hide again. It was an instinct she couldn't push out of her mind.

Her legs moved like she was dragging them through wet concrete instead of over solid ground, but Meg somehow pulled herself through the destroyed garden and into the shadow of it, under the overhang but not inside. The paint was blue and peeling off to show the wood underneath, and it rubbed raw against her back through her dress. It wasn't protecting her much, anymore. The white was turning gray with water and dirt and her bare feet—her sandals were probably in the tunnel, she didn't remember losing them—were coated in dirt. She couldn't even feel them.

The rain flattened her hair against her head, but she hunched back as far as possible and tried to get deep, even breaths into her lungs. This wasn't over yet.

It was beginning to feel like it was never going to be over. She couldn't keep running for much longer.

Meg breathed out. "Tell me what to do," she said out loud. "Come on. What can I *do*?"

Nothing answered her; she wasn't sure what she had expected. She sighed and settled back against the uneven walls of the gazebo. They were rough against her back, when she could feel them at all. She only felt the biggest of the split ends of the wood, the rougher ones that poked into her like needles, because the rest of her skin was untouchably numb. It didn't feel as menacing as the house, even if it was almost as old. It felt like shelter. Maybe because the house had been born of tragedy and this was born of kindness for someone it had killed.

He died out there. We built the gazebo so it couldn't happen again.

The supplies.

Meg jolted around, running her fingers along the wood. The splinter that had pulled at her dress felt different from all the rest. Bigger. When she tugged at it, prying her fingers into the wood even though they burned in protest, the chunk of wood that came off was the diameter of a tent stake—and the rest of the base moved with it. She could barely see the outline of a red gas can inside, a tarp, some shovels, and a small bag.

Yes.

Heart in her throat, Meg pulled out the bag and unzipped it.

Emergency flares. Several of them, brand new, in a water-proof bag. Ones that should burn bright even in the howling wind for someone to see it, and for a good while if it hadn't been raining.

With shaking hands, Meg lifted them up to see the length of cord underneath it, and a fire-starter, and photos, not treated kindly by the elements. They were faded, but on the edges there were intact images: a golden retriever puppy, a white dress, a wave crashing on the shore. Cal and Eliza, smiling broadly, young and showing off Eliza's wedding ring.

There were things about this she was never going to understand.

She couldn't think about it and keep her composure—it would be so *easy* to die, humans were so fragile—but she laid out what she had in front of her. She still had one knife, and the emergency flares... Could she blind him? No, she had to think bigger than that. She had to kill the root of the problem. She had to get someone's attention, from across the forest, and she had to kill Cal.

But to do that, she would need a distraction. She would only have one chance. And she would have to do it face to face. No traps, no hiding, no protection for either of them.

She could live, or she could die. It was that simple. If she didn't stand up, if she waited for Cal to swim back and find a way around, she was going to die. Not abstract, like seeing it on TV, the real thing, the unknown, she was going to feel her own neck snap or her own lungs collapse or—

Meg squeezed her eyes shut, blocking out the things he could do to her, and focused on the possibility so bright she could scarcely stand to think it: she could live. She could beat him at his own game, and survive until morning, and get help.

If she died here, no one would ever know the truth. It would all have been for nothing.

Eliza would be forgotten.

Beth would be dead for nothing.

No.

She took out the flare and held it in her hand, relishing in its sturdiness. In its possibility. It felt like hope.

I'm going to make it, she thought, a last mantra, and went back toward the house.

Chapter Twenty-Nine

Cal found her in five minutes.

He came out the front door, soaking wet but his steps purposeful and calm like he didn't care about nearly drowning in the basement of his house. Maybe the housekeeper had been right when he said the house couldn't hurt him. Maybe he wasn't afraid of dying at all.

She barely saw him, his skin glowing in the faint light cast by the moon, jacket moving in the wind but not enough, like it moved around him instead of through. He walked leisurely, in control, looking right to left, left to right. Scanning. Looking for her, as aware as she was that she couldn't leave without the key in his pocket.

Her hands were shaking. The prey. She felt like the prey, still, for all her planning.

And yet. Right now, she couldn't be. Not anymore. She had to keep him distracted long enough for this to work, to put an end to it.

She lit up the flare in her hand, and its red glare cut through the night like a knife.

Cal turned.

Meg stared across the blackened field at the silhouette, unassuming but deadly, purposeful as it turned to look at her. She knew how she looked through Cal's eyes, because she felt every inch of it: hair still curly but bedraggled and wet, white dress like she was a ghost already dead whipping around her legs, the red glow of the flare painting her stark and desperate against the black night. She looked like a girl out of options, and she was. She looked like she was giving up.

His figure started moving—unhurried, without hiding, not even bothering to stalk her.

Meg's hand tightened around the flare, taking comfort in its light.

For the dead.

For me.

She wasn't going to die here. She watched him come like it was happening to someone else, like she was outside of her body, and everything fell together with every move. Her choices mattered, still, more than ever, but the universe was already in motion. She was close enough to look at him and see him in the dim light of her flare. He seemed like someone different. Too clean, for all the blood he had spilled tonight.

His every step toward her, she felt through her bones like an echo. Cal wasn't a person now. He was dangerous—a predator.

She took a step backwards too. She was three steps from the cliff, from dying. The flare in her hand didn't feel like a weapon at all.

"It didn't have to be like this," he said, so quietly she almost didn't hear him over the wind. There was still a chilling conviction in his eyes. "I could have let you live."

Meg's rage was so thick it felt tangible. "I don't want your mercy," she said. "You're a murderer. I want you to pay for it."

Cal swallowed, pursed his lips, and then took another step toward her. Meg took another step back.

Two paces.

"You remind me of her," he whispered. "Of Eliza. You don't look like her, but you... feel the same." He paused, took another step forward that was so subtle that Meg almost missed her own step back. One pace.

"You have the same eyes," he said quietly. "You look at me the same way."

And he seemed almost confused by it, and a last piece of the puzzle clicked into place: Eliza had known what kind of person Cal was, at one point, and she had either pushed it away or made herself forget that fear. That was why she died.

"Is that why you killed her?" Meg asked. "Because she seemed happy. She seemed like... she loved you."

Cal's eyes fixed on her, but beyond her as well. There was something there, some memory he was trying to suppress and dig up at the same time... but then it flickered out and died, suddenly and completely, and it was just Cal staring at her. Cal the murderer who everyone else believed was just a man.

She was so close. Her heart was going to beat out of her chest. So close.

"You *killed her*," Meg said. She wanted him to know that, to know what it meant.

"What are you hoping to accomplish with this?" he asked with an edge of amusement.

The *rage*. She was shaking with that, not fear anymore.

"Stalling," she whispered as the countdown in her head reached zero.

There was a deafening roar, too close to be thunder but just as primordial, and Cal ducked and clapped his hands over his ears but Meg was ready for it. While his back was turned, the flare went from her right hand to her left. With her right, she drew the knife.

Behind them, over Cal's head as he spun around and straightened in disbelief, the house was burning. Burning bright as a solar flare on the sun in spite of the wind and the rain, spurred on by the emergency gas, started from the extra flare and the photos of Cal and Eliza that were dry, inside a house that still carried the memory of burning down. The flames licked up the sides, through the windows with the glass blown out and scattered on the ground, up the peeling painted sides; inside, a beam came down with a snap like bone. The smoke that came toward her, whipped up by the wind, was salty and dry and deep black, and smelled of flesh and pine.

The whole house groaned, like it was crying out, and the inside of it collapsed all at once. Fractured, like the sound in her memory that played whenever she closed her eyes. *Crack.* And then nothing.

Like things dying.

The noise that came out of Cal's mouth was something primal, full of rage and grief and denial—tearing out of deep in his throat and gut, like when Kendra had leaped at him to strangle him for her dead husband—and Meg knew what he was going to do even before he turned on his heel and closed the distance between them like a wolf pouncing on prey. Instinct. Drive. So much rage you had to turn it into motion.

She was ready.

She let him crash into her and plunged the knife into his stomach.

Too shallow. He didn't stop moving, didn't even hitch in his screaming, and she dropped it and reached for the edge as they fell over the side of the cliff.

Meg had expected rock under her fingernails; what she got was crumbling dirt. And then Cal seized onto her leg, and the weight of it dragged her backwards and down. Her face went to the sky, the rain washing relentlessly into her eyes, and she gasped and held on. There was one rock, under her right hand, and that kept her upright when everything else was turning to mud under the water.

Her hold on the edge of the cliff was slipping, but she could feel, where Cal was holding onto her, that it was slick. His grip was strong but she would outlast him. She would outlast him or she would stab him again in the throat or she would kick him off of her but she *would not die.*

There was another shriek from the house, a beam snapping in two. A roof caving in. A hundred years of blood leaching up and into the sky.

And Cal let go of her and fell. Silently. Like he was already dead.

She gasped and swung her hands up and over the edge of the cliff, grasping the grass blades between her fingers.

Alive.

Meg crawled up, one clawed handhold at a time. She was grateful for the wind and rain that buffeted her ears. One crunch of bone on rocks was enough for a lifetime. She didn't need to look down to know how it would appear in the tiny bit of light on the beach.

But she was alive.

She shivered and waited for the sun to rise as the house burned to a dull orange glow in front of her.

CHAPTER THIRTY

There were things, in the morning, when the sun came up, when the police and the fire trucks and the news reporters arrived, that Meg had no answers to.

The crow, with its limp broken neck, wasn't found in the tunnels. Neither was Beth's body. The best guess was that they had been reduced to ash when the floorboards burned. Maybe boiled to nothing. Meg expected to throw up, when they told her that, she expected it to trigger a last bout of rage, but she had nothing left in her. Their bones were gone. There was nothing left to bury.

When they recovered Jay and Kendra's bodies, so close together it looked like they had been reaching for each other as they died separately, she could smell it. Their faces looked plastic; the flesh had been burnt off so badly it was melting down their chins like crash dummies doused in gasoline. Kendra's badge wasn't recovered. It had been lost in the fire, too, which was a shame. Meg wanted to tell them where she had last seen it, which room had been hers, but her 'room' was in a pile of tinder with the rest and she had no words anyway.

Why?

Everyone kept asking her that. The onlookers, the emergency crews, the reporters, the police officers who wondered how she survived when one of their own had perished. Why had she done it? Was she brave? Was she stupid? Suicidal?

Why did he do it?

There was no one left who knew. His father, maybe, but he was dead and the truth was dead with him. The groundskeeper, maybe, missing or dead too, who saw so much and couldn't help her either, if he was even there. She wasn't sure, anymore.

Was the house really haunted?

Her neck burned, like it had left its brand on her, a ring of skin rubbed raw that she was lucky hadn't crushed her windpipe. But she wasn't lucky. Cal had saved her.

The house is only dangerous to those who are dangerous to me.

It was true that Cal was a murderer. But it was also true that there were things about this she was never going to understand.

How did you find the videos? Who put them at that garage sale for you to find?

She didn't need to understand. Some stories were better without endings.

Meg closed her eyes to the house, its blackened fallen bones crumbling to ash in the wind and filling her nose; the edge of the cliff, dipping off into nothing, abrupt as death; the gray rising ocean crashing against the rocks where Cal's body was still in pieces, still not recovered because the tide was in and the riptide was killer; the sunrise like fire blooming over the horizon; the beat of the waves and the salt of the air and the wind in her dress and the taste of dirt in her mouth disappearing in streaks behind the air she breathed until they faded to dull memories.

She was alive.

And if she thought she smelled roses, or heard her name on the wind, it was lost in the crash of the waves on the rocks.

Acknowledgements

Thanks firstly to my ever-patient family, who have been supportive from the very beginning. Thank you for always encouraging me to write, for listening as I talked through endless plot points and logistics and rewrites. It means so much to finally share the finished story with you after just telling you about it for so long. Love you lots!

Thank you so much to Lauren and Allison, my amazing writing group. You guys have read this book SO MANY TIMES and gave me so much good feedback and advice, and without your constant support this book wouldn't exist. I can't wait to have tons more crazy writing sleepovers and parties and zoom calls with you. You're the best writing buddies I could ever ask for!

Thank you, Kristina, for being one of the first people to support me in my goal to publish. Your sweet messages and enthusiasm have encouraged me and kept me pushing to finish. Hope it's worth the wait!

There are too many to put down by name, but thanks also to everyone I told who encouraged me to finish this and publish it. If you were one of them who promised to look up my book in a year when it was ready, asked for a signed copy when I was done, gave me a piece of advice or pointed me towards someone who could help: thank you. It helped more than you could ever imagine.

And finally, a huge thank you to you for reading! Meg's story was a labor of love and has meant so much to me for so long, but hopefully it's only the first of many. I have more ideas for stories than there are hours in the day to write them, and I look forward to sharing them all with you.

About the Author

ALEXA DONLEY writes a little of everything, but she has a special love for stories about magic. She lives in Federal Way, Washington, and when she's not writing, she likes traveling to new places and walking in thunderstorms.

For more of her work, visit www.alexadonley.com.

www.ingramcontent.com/pod-product-compliance
Lightning Source LLC
Chambersburg PA
CBHW020022310726
48970CB00007B/2164